### "WHITE INDIAN"

The earth was wide. The sky was the spread
wings of a giant bluebird. The hated prison
of the white man's houses, the white man's
clothing, lay far behind. Soon True Son
would be with his cousin, Half Arrow,
deep in the Indian forest.

But now he heard horses behind him, and suddenly
his white father and his Uncle Wilse, the man
who hated Indians and butchered them
without mercy, rode upon either side of him.
"Liar, thief!" Uncle Wilse said.

His white father looked at True Son anxiously.
"Johnny," he said. "Johnny." True Son held
himself quietly, as an Indian should,
though his heart thudded against his ribs.
He knew he must go with them now, but someday
he would again be free . . .

---

"Rebellion, glowing vitality . . . the spirit of
the wild frontier . . . Absorbing story,
marked by Mr. Richter's uncanny skill
in recapturing the atmosphere of the past."

NEW YORK TIMES

# THE LIGHT
# IN THE FOREST

## CONRAD RICHTER

**BANTAM BOOKS**
TORONTO • NEW YORK • LONDON • SYDNEY • AUCKLAND

RL 4, IL age 12 and up

THE LIGHT IN THE FOREST
*A Bantam Book / published by arrangement with
Alfred A. Knopf, Inc.*

PRINTING HISTORY
*Knopf edition published May 1953
Five printings through February 1956*
*Serialized in* SATURDAY EVENING POST *March-April 1953*
*Lutheran Reader's Club edition published September 1953*
*Bantam edition / November 1954
New Bantam edition / May 1958
8 printings through July 1962
Bantam Pathfinder edition / February 1968
42 printings through October 1974
Bantam edition / September 1975
35 printings through September 1984*

ISBN 0-553-24907-X

*Published simultaneously in the United States and Canada*

*Bantam Books are published by Bantam Books, Inc. Its trade-
mark consisting of the words "Bantam Books" and the por-
trayal of a rooster, is Registered in U.S. Patent and Trademark
Office and in other countries. Marca Registrada. Bantam
Books, Inc., 666 Fifth Avenue, New York, New York 10103.*

Shades of the prison-house begin to close
    Upon the growing Boy,
But he beholds the light, and whence it flows,
    He sees it in his joy.

—WORDSWORTH

## ACKNOWLEDGMENTS

The author acknowledges his debt to Heckewelder's *Indian Nations;* to Zeisberger's *History of North American Indians;* and to many other early volumes made available by Miss Nell B. Stevens, acting director of the Pennsylvania state library; by Miss Alice R. Eaton, librarian of the Harrisburg, Pennsylvania, public library; and by Walter B. Kuhn of the library of the University of New Mexico; also to the counsel of Paul A. W. Wallace, editor of *Pennsylvania History,* who read the manuscript and furnished material; to Anthony F. C. Wallace of the University of Pennsylvania, who made suggestions; to Donald H. Kent, associate Pennsylvania state historian, who furnished photostats of early maps and manuscripts; and to many others who lent aid and encouragement.

The author wants to acknowledge further his gratitude to those readers who have sensed what he was trying to do—not to write historical novels but to give an authentic sensation of life in early America. In records of the Eastern border, the author was struck by the numbers of returned white captives who tried desperately to run away from their flesh-and-blood families and return to their Indian foster homes and the Indian mode of life. As a small boy he himself had tried to run off to Indian country without the benefit of ever having lived among the savages.

Not that the novel represents the novelist's particular beliefs or opinions. He can understand and sympathize with either side. His business is to be fair to them both. If the novel has another purpose, it is to point out that in the pride of our American liberties, we're apt to forget that already we've lost a good many to civilization. The American Indians once enjoyed far more than we. Already two hundred years ago, when restrictions were comparatively with us, our ideals and restrained manner of existence repelled the Indian. I thought that perhaps if we understood how these First Americans felt toward us even then and toward our white way of life, we might better understand the adverse, if perverted, view of us by some African, European, and Asian peoples today.

*i*

THE BOY was about fifteen years old. He tried to stand very straight and still when he heard the news, but inside of him everything had gone black. It wasn't that he couldn't endure pain. In summer he would put a stone hot from the fire on his flesh to see how long he could stand it. In winter he would sit in the icy river until his Indian father smoking on the bank said he could come out. It made him strong against any hardship that would come to him, his father said. But if it had any effect on this thing that had come to him now, the boy couldn't tell what it was.

For days word had been reaching the Indian village that the Lenni Lenape and Shawanose must give up their white prisoners. Never for a moment did the boy dream that it meant him. Why, he had been one of them since he could remember! Cuyloga was his father. Eleven years past he had been adopted to take the place of a son dead from the yellow vomit. More than once he had been told how, when he was only four years old, his father had said words that took out his white blood and put Indian blood in its place. His white thoughts and meanness had been wiped away and the brave

1

thoughts of the Indian put in their stead. Ever since, he had been True Son, the blood of Cuyloga and flesh of his flesh. For eleven years he had lived here, a native of this village on the Tuscarawas, a full member of the family. Then how could he be torn from his home like a sapling from the ground and given to the alien whites who were his enemy!

The day his father told him, the boy made up his mind. Never would he give up his Indian life. Never! When no one saw him, he crept away from the village. From an old campfire, he blackened his face. Up above Pockhapockink, which means the stream between two hills, he had once found a hollow tree. Now he hid himself in it. He thought only he knew the existence of that tree and was dismayed when his father tracked him to it. It was humiliating to be taken back with his blackened face and tied up in his father's cabin like some prisoner to be burned at the stake. When his father led him out next morning, he knew everybody watched: his mother and sisters, the townspeople, his uncle and aunt, his cousins and his favorite cousin, Half Arrow, with whom he had ever fished, hunted and played. Seldom had they been separated even for a single day.

All morning on the path with his father, crazy thoughts ran like squirrels in the boy's head. Never before had he known his father to be in the wrong. Could it be that he was in the right now? Had he unknowingly left a little white blood in the boy's veins and was it for this that he must be returned? Then they came in sight of the ugly log redoubts and pale tents of the white army, and the boy felt sure there was in his body not a drop of blood that knew these things. At the sight and smells of the white man, strong aversion and loathing came over him. He tried with all his young strength to get away. His father had to hold him hard. In the end he dragged him twisting and yelling over the ground to the council house of the whites and threw him on the leaves that had been spread around.

"I gave talking paper that I bring him," he told the white guards. "Now he belong to you."

It was all over then, the boy knew. He was as good as dead and lay among the other captives with his face down. He was sure that his father had stayed. He could feel his presence and smell the sweet inner bark of the red willow mixed with the dried sumach leaves of his pipe. When dusk fell, a white guard came up. The other soldiers called him Del, perhaps because he could talk Delaware, the strange name the whites gave the Lenni Lenape and their languages. True Son heard Del tell his father that all Indians must be out of the camp by nightfall. From the sounds the boy guessed his father was knocking out his pipe and putting it away. Then he knew he had risen and was standing over him.

"Now go like an Indian, True Son," he said in a low, stern voice. "Give me no more shame."

He left almost at once and the boy heard his footsteps in the leaves. The rustling sound grew farther and farther away. When he sat up, his father was gone. But never before or since was the place his father was going back to so clear and beautiful in the boy's mind. He could see the great oaks and shiver-bark hickories standing over the village in the autumn dusk, the smoke rising from the double row of cabins with the street between, and the shining, white reflection of the sky in the Tuscarawas beyond. Fallen red, brown and golden leaves lay over roofs and bushes, street and forest floor. Tramping through them could be made out the friendly forms of those he knew, warriors and hunters, squaws, and the boys, dogs and girls he had played with. Through the open door of his father's cabin shone the warm red fire with his mother and sisters over it, for this was the beginning of the Month of the First Snow,

November. Near the fire heavy bark had been strewn on the ground, and on it lay his familiar bed and the old worn half-grown bearskin he pulled over himself at night. Homesickness overwhelmed him, and he sat there and wept.

After a while he was conscious of eyes upon him. When he looked up, he saw the white guard they called Del, standing there in the dusk that to the Indian is part of the day and part of the night. The white soldier was about twenty years old, with red hair and a hunting shirt of some coarse brownish cloth. The bosom stuck out like a pouch from his belongings carried in it. His belt was tied in the back and his cape fringed with threads that in the daylight were raveled scarlet and green. But what affronted the boy was that the white guard laughed at him.

Instantly True Son turned and lay on his face again. Inside of him hate rose like a poison.

"Once my hands are loose, I'll get his knife," he promised himself. "Then quickly I'll kill him."

*ii*

WHEN Del Hardy had left Fort Pitt in October, he reckoned he was looking on the Allegheny River for the last time. It was his first stint with the army and his only one with Colonel Bouquet. Afterwards he was to serve under Generals Sullivan, Broadhead and Wayne, but Bouquet was the one he claimed he'd go through hell for the willingest. The Colonel was the peacefullest man, Del used to say, but mad as a wolverine. He marched his men out of Fort Pitt that fall day like they were going to a celebration.

And what was the celebration? Why, they were setting out on a suicide march! They were heading more than a hundred miles into hostile Indian territory! Mind you, this was plumb wilderness, with no roads, and no forts or white settlements to fall back on. Every day the savages would be lying thick as copper snakes in the woods around them. The whites would be outnumbered two to one, maybe worse. And yet the peace-palavering Colonel swore he wouldn't halt till he'd reach the Forks of the Muskingum, which only a few of his men had ever seen.

Del never expected to reach those Forks alive. Nor

did a lot of older and more seasoned men. But the Colonel looked after them like they were his own sons. He marched them in matching lines to protect each other, with the pack horses and stock in the middle. He let no man on the march bandy words with his neighbor. All day he kept ordering Del and the others to be on guard against ambush. But his hardest order was that, unless attacked, they hadn't dare lay hands on a savage.

"Mind you," Del liked to tell later, "half of us were volunteers. We had risked our hair with him for one reason. We'd lost kin captured or scalped, and our one idea was to get them back or get back at the Injuns. When we came to Injun sign or towns, our fingers itched like fire on our hatchets and triggers. We cursed the Colonel's orders right and left. But that's as far as we went. We never touched hair nor hide of those Injun hostages we had marchin' beside us, though we knew the devils had scalped plenty of our people in their time."

Del couldn't believe it when they got there. But according to them that knew, this miserable spot in the wilderness was the wonderful, Indian-sacred Forks of the Muskingum. There from the northeast came the Tuscarawas. Yonder from the northwest the Waldhoning, or White Woman's River, flowed into it. And now when they were so deep in Indian country it looked as if they'd never get out, the Colonel got doughtier and spunkier than ever. He sassed back the Indian messengers who came into camp. He said they could have no peace till they'd bring in their white prisoners.

"I told the Colonel they'd never give in on that," Del said. "I'd lived with the Delawares my own self when I was little, and I told him if white prisoners weren't killed right off, they were adopted, mostly for some dead relative. They were made brother or sister or son or daughter or wife. It wasn't any mock or make-believe business either. Those Injuns actually looked on their new white relations like full-blooded Injuns. And they'd never give them up any more than their own people."

Del used to rub his chin.

"But I was plumb wrong. They hated to give them up all right. But they hated worse to see a white man's town a settin' there on the banks of their own river. They hated like poison the sight of our tents and redoubts. They couldn't wait to clear out our axes from cuttin' down their Injun woods and our cattle from eatin' the grass on their river bottoms. They were scared we were takin' over the country. So they started fetchin' in their white relations."

That was a sight Del Hardy never would forget. The Colonel himself rubbed his eyes to find savages, whose names were a terror on the frontier, crying like women as they gave up some white child or wife. They held to them, gave them presents to take along and begged the white captain to be good to them. But what many of the men couldn't get over was the ungratefulness of the captives. They didn't want to have anything to do with the whites who had risked their lives to rescue them. They called out in Delaware to their Indian masters to take them back again to their Indian homes.

Of all the prisoners Del saw brought in, the fifteen-year-old boy from Pennsylvania was the wildest and most rebellious. He had to be tied up with strips of buffalo hide, and then he struggled like a panther kit trussed up on a pole. His name in Delaware, his father said, was True Son, but never had Del seen anybody so unwilling to go back to his true father and mother.

Del had gone up to the North Tuscarawas redoubt when he first saw the pair on the path. The boy wore a brand-new calico hunting shirt, probably made by his mother and sisters for the occasion to show they could dress him as well as the whites. It covered the boy's upper parts and half way down his leggings. His hair was black and his face and arms brown as an Indian's, but you couldn't mistake the English cast of his features. He was plainly white, and yet when he came in sight of the white camp, he stopped dead, a wild expression flew in his face, and he fought like a bobcat to get away. Squaws and Indian children who had come with other prisoners watched and stared. Their faces never moved a muscle, but you could tell they understood and felt for the prisoner.

When Del got back to duty at the council house, the boy lay flat on his face. After dark when the fires burned low, the guard caught him tearing with his teeth at the knots that bound him.

"If you know what's good for you, you won't try to get away!" he warned sharply in Delaware.

The boy turned on him.

"I spit on white people!" he told him.

"Don't forget you're white your own self," Del retorted.

"I'm Indian!" the boy said and looked up at him straight in the eye. The guard didn't laugh. There were times when Indian feelings still came up in him strong.

"Well, your father and mother were white anyway," Del tried to reason with him.

"My father is Cuyloga. My mother, Quaquenga," he said.

"Yes, lately. But you had another father and mother before them. The ones you were born to."

"Nobody can help how he is born," he informed with dignity.

"You can argue like an Injun all right," Del agreed. "But your skin is still white."

"You call this white?" He held out his arm.

"Let's see the skin under that shirt." But the boy hit

savagely at the extended hand. He wouldn't let the guard touch him.

"You've been away from us a long time," Del soothed him. "When you're back in our country a while, you'll get used to us."

"I'll never go back to your country."

"It's your country, too."

"This is my country!" he called out with such passion that Del shrugged his shoulders and walked away.

By daylight, True Son still lay on his face.

"You better get up and eat." Del nudged him with the toe of his moccasin.

The boy shrank with loathing.

"*Palli aal!* Go away."

"You got to eat. You can't tramp back to Pennsylvania on air."

"I'll never go back to Pennsylvania."

"Then where do you reckon you're goin'?"

"A place where you can't tramp me with your big foot."

Now what did the young varmint mean by that, Del wondered. But the boy closed his mouth and would not say more.

**iii**

THE THIRD day a change came among the tents and
log redoubts along the Tuscarawas. The camp quick-
ened. You could close your eyes and feel the nervous
bustle and excitation of the white man. Soldiers moved
quick-step at their task. They called lively to each other
and hummed strange-sounding ditties.

"Does it mean something?" True Son asked a captive
who knew all the talk of the Yengwes.

"Tomorrow we leave for Pennsylvania," she told him.

That day the boy lay with despair in his breast. His
life had been short but now it must come to its end.
Never would he go to this enemy land. How could he
exist among a race of aliens with such slouching ways
and undignified speech! How could he live and breathe
and not be an Indian!

He would have to act now. He remembered his
father's friend, Make Daylight, who lived in the next
village. Make Daylight had been forsaken, too. His
squaw had gone to another Indian's cabin to live. She
had taken Make Daylight's children with her. Make
Daylight had stood his abandonment and disgrace a few
days. Then he went in the forest and ate the root of the

May apple. He had been brave in war. No one thought him a coward now. So no one would think True Son a coward when they found him lying silent and superior to the white man. They would say True Son had triumphed over his enemies. Never could they carry him off to Pennsylvania now. No, his body would stay in his beloved land along the Tuscarawas. Word would be sent to Cuyloga, his father. Through the village the mourning cry would pass. "He is no more!" His father and mother, his sisters, his uncle and aunt and cousins would come to him. They would put logs and posts on the fresh earth against the wolves. Under the ground near his head they would set good Lenni Lenape food to feed him on his journey.

Three times that day the boy tried to get the root of the May apple. His white guard, Del, gave him no chance. When he went from the council house, the guard kept hold of him like a haltered beast. He would have to wait till he was on the march. Some time tomorrow they would pass through a wooded meadow. At the place of the May apple he would fall to the ground. When they lifted him up, he would have the death medicine in his hands.

It was a gray morning when they left the Forks of the Muskingum. For a while their way lay on the path by which the boy and his father had come. True Son's heart rose. It was almost as if he were going home. When they came to the parting of the trails, something in him wanted to cry out. An ancient sycamore stood at the forks, one dead limb pointing to the gloomy trace to Pennsylvania. On the far side, a live branch indicated the path running bright and free toward home. The boy's moccasins wanted to race on that path. He could feel himself light as a deer leaping over roots and logs, through the deep woods, over the hills and by the nar-

rows to the village on the bank of the Tuscarawas.
Violently he struggled to escape, but the guard pushed
him on.

Through the blackness in his heart, he heard a voice
calling in Delaware.

"True Son! Look! Not yonder. I am here."

The boy's eyes found a young Indian in leggings,
breech clout and strouding. He was moving in the woods
abreast of him. Never had he believed that such a feeling of joy and hope would sweep over him again. He
would know that form anywhere.

"Is it you, Half Arrow? Do you still live?" he called.

"No, it's Between-the-Logs," Half Arrow called back
in delight, for Between-the-Logs was very old and lame
and that was a joke between them. "I wait a long time.
I think you never come. Then you come but I see you
bound up. How is such a thing? I thought you were
among friends and your people!"

"I am not among my people, but my enemies," the
boy said bitterly.

"Well, anyway, I am your people and am with you,"
his cousin cheered him. "If Little Crane marches with
his white squaw, I can march with you and keep you
company."

"I cannot believe it. What will my father say?"

"He says plenty, but let's talk of pleasant and cheerful
things. How we can kill these white devils so you can
come back to the village with me."

"*Jukella!* If only I could! But there are too many for
us."

"The more they are, the more scalps and loot we
get!" Half Arrow declared eagerly.

"*Sehe!* Watch out. Some can understand our language," True Son warned him, but Half Arrow laughed,
and True Son knew he was talking as he always did,
just for Indian cheerfulness and companionship, half in

joke and half in earnest, but mostly in joke, for there were nearly two thousand armed white men, and not all the Delaware and Shawanose warriors in the woods had dared attack them.

Most of the day Half Arrow kept up his talking and calling to him. The pair had been apart for three days, and now his chatter ran on to make up for it. All the time he talked he kept tirelessly leaping over rocks and logs and brushing limbs aside. To see and hear him did True Son good like medicine. It seemed an age since he had heard an Indian joke and seen a dark face break into a wonderful Indian smile. Even Little Crane went sad as a bear near his white bride. But Half Arrow was bright and full of village and family news.

True Son did not notice now when they passed the bare and withered stalks of the May apple. At midday he could even joke a little.

"Half Arrow. Come out of the woods. You're burned too red for the white man to want to take back to Pennsylvania."

"But not too red to shoot me and take my scalp back," Half Arrow said quickly.

"They could have shot you any time all day," True Son pointed out.

"Yes, but not so easy. They might have missed me with all the trees and bushes between. They are poor shots anyway, especially at Indians who jump and dance. But if I came in close to you like a cousin, they could reach me with their tomahawks and long knives."

"They haven't tomahawked Little Crane."

"Well, then, in that case I'll take a chance on the white devils," Half Arrow said and started to edge a little nearer. When at last he came cautiously out of the timber onto the trace, True Son looked with interest at the pack on his back, although it wasn't polite to acknowledge its existence. Half Arrow ate greedily the

bread True Son shared with him. At the same time he
made a wry grimace over the meat.

"What kind of flesh is this they give you?"

"White man's beef."

"So that's why they're so pale and bandy-legged," he
nodded, "having to eat such old and stringy leather
while Indian people have rich venison and bear meat."

All afternoon the two cousins marched together, and
at times True Son could almost forget the bitterness of
his destination. At supper they ate together, but the red-
haired guard would not let them sleep side by side. You
couldn't trust an Indian. Half Arrow would have to go
off in the woods by himself to sleep, like Little Crane.

"I will sleep in the wood," Half Arrow said with dignity. "But first I bear presents to my cousin." He lifted
from his pack a small buckskin sack of parched corn. It
was so True Son would go well-fed with the whites and
remember his uncle who sent it. After that, he fetched
out moccasins embroidered in red by True Son's mother
and sisters so he would go back to his white people
newly shod and remember his mother and sisters. Fi-
nally all that was left of the pack was its covering, the
old worn bearskin that had been True Son's bed in the
cabin.

"Your father sent it so you could go warm at night to
your white people and remember your father," Half
Arrow told him.

In a concealed rush of emotion, True Son held it up in
his hands. With the feel of it against his body and the
familiar smell of it in his nostrils, he could almost believe that he was back home again in the beloved cabin.

"But what will you have on such a cold night for
yourself?" he asked.

"Me! I'll have plenty and more!" Half Arrow boasted.
"I have my strouding. Then I'll scrape myself a hill of
leaves, yes a whole mountain to crawl inside of. I'll have

a soft bed of leaves below me and a thick blanket of sweet-smelling leaves above me. I'll bounce and flex my muscles till I sweat. Then I'll be snug and warm as Zelozelos, the cricket, in a wigwam."

## iv

ALL the way to the ominous-sounding Fort Pitt, True Son tried to keep his mind from the gloomy hour when Half Arrow must turn back and leave him. Only rarely did his cousin mention it.

"I think now I have tramped enough toward the sun's rising," he would soberly begin the subject.

True Son would put on a strained and formal face.

"Yes, tomorrow you must go back. *Elkesa!* What does your father say?"

"He doesn't say because he doesn't know how far I am," Half Arrow would remind him.

"He knows you're not home yet."

"Yes, but he knows Little Crane must come back too, and we can travel together."

"Little Crane might not come back. He's lovesick for his white squaw. He would like to stay with her."

"Then I'll go back by myself. Never could I get lost on such a wide road. All I need do is follow horse droppings."

"Some white devil might ambush you."

"Never could he hit me," Half Arrow boasted. "When

16

he shoots, I jump. Let me hear his rifle, and Achto, the deer, has no legs like mine. Ten jumps from campsite to campsite. My feet won't even get in the rivers. I'll fly over, like Ploeu, the turkey."

Now that the subject of Half Arrow's return had been duly mentioned, it could be put away till another time. To keep it covered up and out of sight, they talked of many things. One was the respective qualities of the white men's horses and which ones they would steal and ride home on if they got the chance. Another pleasant subject was the white guards they disliked and with what strokes, if they met them alone in the woods, they would kill and scalp them.

Sometimes Little Crane left his white squaw to walk with the cousins, and then they talked of the foolish ways of the white people.

"The reason they act so queer," Little Crane pointed out, "is because they're not an original people. Now we Indians are an original people. The Great Being made us from the beginning. Look! Our hair is always black, our eyes and skin dark, even True Son's here. But the whites are of colors like horses. Some are light, some are dark, some are in-between. Some have black hair, some have light hair. Some have hair the color of a rotting log. Some have hair like the Colonel's horse, and some have even red like his blanket. Their eyes are fickle as their hair. It's because they are a mixed people, and that's what makes them so foolish and troublesome. The Great Being knows their disposition. He had to give them a Good Book and teach them to read so they could learn what is good and bad. Now we Indians know good and bad for ourselves without a book or the cumbersome labor of reading."

"I think," Half Arrow said, "they are all near-sighted. Do you notice how when we come upon them they crowd close to stare at us? They almost tread on our toes. Now an Indian's eyes are keen and far-sighted. He can stand at a distance and see all that he wants to."

"They must be hard of hearing too," True Son mentioned. "They talk loud though they stand close enough to each other to touch with a stick."

"And they all talk at once like waterfowl," Half Arrow declared. "How can they understand what is being said? Why don't their elders teach them to keep silent and listen till the speaker's done?"

"It's because they're such a new people," Little Crane explained. "They are young and heedless like children. You can see it the way they heap up treasures like a child, although they know they must die and can't take such things with them. It would be no use anyhow because the next world has plenty of everything a man wants. Their house isn't big enough for all they gather, so they have to build another house they call the barn. That's why you find so many thieves among the whites. All white people must put what they call a lock on their door. It's made of iron and you must carry another piece of iron with you to open it."

"If they shared with their brothers like the Indian, they wouldn't have the work of building a second house," Half Arrow said. "Don't they see the sense of this?"

"Oh, they're a peculiar race and no sensible man can understand them," Little Crane answered. "Have you never noticed them on the march? What do we Indians look for? We look for game or tracks or how the Great Being made our country beautiful with trees for the forest, water for the river, and grass for the prairies. But the white man sees little of this. He looks mostly at the ground. He digs it up with his iron tool to see how black and deep it goes. Sometimes he makes a fuss of the trees. He says, look, here are walnut and hickory and cherry and white ash and locust and sugar trees. But it's not for the trees, only because the ground is black and deep that such trees stand in. Yet if there is much white oak and beech, that feed the squirrels and bear and turkey, he makes a face. He says such country is good for nothing."

"I've noticed the white men's foolishness in the woods," Half Arrow nodded. "When the time grows near to camp for the night, they keep their eyes half closed. They don't look for a high and dry place but set themselves down in any wet and dirty place, just so it's under some big trees. They don't even look which way the wind blows before they make their campfire. When the smoke blows on them, they try to hit it with their hands and caps like mosquitoes."

"*Bischik!*" True Son agreed. "And they hang their kettles right away before the blackest of the smoke has passed. They burn any kind of wood that's handy. Green oak or cherry or walnut or chestnut that throws many sparks. You can see their blankets and clothing always have holes burned in them."

"All you say is true," Little Crane declared. "But one thing they do I would not like to change. That's the way they lie down at night. They never look up first to see if heavy dead branches hang over their heads. Some time I hope the Great Being sends a big wind to knock down the dead wood and kill them in their beds."

The three laughed. True Son didn't know what he would do when Half Arrow and Little Crane weren't there to keep him company. And now there were signs that they wouldn't be with him long. A Mohawk from the north fell in with them that day. He said soon they would meet a large river and that Fort Pitt was on this river. The very next day it happened as he said, but the waters were swollen with rains. They would have to wait for the flood to go down before crossing.

Next morning when Half Arrow and Little Crane came back from the forest, they found the body of the Mohawk near camp. He had been tomahawked and scalped. Now a Delaware sheds no tears for a Mingo, and especially a Mohawk, but though dogs may fight among themselves they are one against the wolf.

"I think white soldiers did this," Little Crane said. "One of them made friendly talk to him in front. Another came up and tomahawked him from behind."

Inside of him, True Son felt bitterness for all the white soldiers. The Mohawk might be ugly, but he was an Indian. It was hard to hold in his feelings next morning when the red-haired guard said that this was the day True Son and Half Arrow must part. In a little while they would be crossing the river, and his cousin must stay on this side.

"Why do you spit on my cousin?" True Son asked.

"Little Crane can't come either. We're getting close to white people now. Some of them have suffered from the Indians and might kill him."

"They could kill him just as easy on this side, like they did the Mohawk."

"It's the Colonel's orders."

"He's not Half Arrow's colonel. Why does he have to obey him?"

The guard flushed. He said nothing more. But when the column started to move toward the ford, he took his rifle and, holding it at Half Arrow's breast, forced him out of line. True Son felt fresh hate for the white man. His arms had been freed to let him carry his pack above the water. Now he dropped his belongings and made a lunge at the guard. He knocked him down, tried to pull out first the guard's knife and then his hatchet. Over the ground they rolled, while a second soldier drew a bead on Half Arrow and others came running to pull True Son off.

"You Injun-crazy young fool!" the red-haired guard panted as he got up. "I wasn't trying to shoot him—just to save his hair."

As they tied his arms again True Son still struggled. Half Arrow stood by, grave and impassive.

"Once long ago my cousin had white blood," he apologized to the guard. "Now you can rest your mind. I will stay on this side like you say. But first I would like to give True Son a message from his father before we are separated by the waters."

"You can give him a message," the guard said sharply. "But don't try to give him a knife. If you do, you'll get a bullet between your ribs."

At the order to march Half Arrow moved beside True Son. Through the trees ahead they could see the river. "I talk now for your father, True Son," he began. "He said I should tell you this. On no account must I forget. These are his words: 'True Son. Remember what happens to the white prisoner the Indian takes. If the white prisoner bears his hardship with patience and cheerfulness, his Indian master likes him. He knows he will make a good Indian. So he treats him well and adopts him. True Son. If the white prisoner fights him or hangs back or tries to escape or if he complains all the time, the Indian knows he will never make one like himself. Then there is nothing to do but scalp him. True Son. If you fight and hang back, maybe the white man will scalp you. True Son. It is better to wait for your cause to be ripe like a persimmon on the snow before you fight back. True Son. It is wiser to be willing and be alive than be defiant and be dead so your father and mother and sisters have to mourn you.'"

True Son bowed his head. The words were so like his father's, he could hear the sound of his father's voice in his mind. Half Arrow went on.

"Your father said more. He said, 'True Son. Remem-

ber the time we hunted on the White Woman's River?
We came on a bear and the shot broke its backbone. The
bear fell down and started to cry like Long Tail, the
panther.' Your father went up and struck it with his ram-
rod across the nose. He said, 'Listen, bear. You are a
coward and not the warrior you pretend to be. You know
our tribes are at war. Had you conquered me, I would
have borne it with courage and died like a warrior. But
you, bear, sit and whimper like an old woman. You disgrace your tribe with your behavior.' True Son. Do you
remember?"

"I remember," the boy groaned. "Tell my father so.
Tell him I will bear my disgrace like an Indian and will
wait to strike till the time is in my favor."

The two marched on in silence. When they came to
the river's edge, Half Arrow stepped aside and True
Son waded in alone. The water grew steadily higher
till it reached above his waist. He shivered, but he did
not turn around. Not until he was out and dripping on
the other side and following the trail on the bank with
the column did he look back. Far across the water he
could make out two figures. They were Half Arrow and
Little Crane, standing at the water's edge. Their eyes,
he knew, strained after him. He wished he could hold
up his hand in farewell but his arms were tied. Then he
passed with his companions into the forest.

*v*

FROM now forward he was on his own, the boy told himself. He would have to think his own Indian thoughts and follow his own Indian counsel. He gave no sign of the constriction in his throat or the loathing in his breast when they entered the white man's stronghold of Fort Pitt; the gloomy stone, the dark passageways, the drunken soldiers, all the swaggering of the white-skinned legion and among them a few turncoat Indians looking pitiful and slavish among their enemies.

But it was when they had left Fort Pitt and crossed the eastern mountains that the full weight of his exile fell on him. Never along the Tuscarawas had he seen such tremendous mounds of earth and rock heaped to the sky and running farther than the eye could see. Once behind him, they were like unscalable stockades separating him from his people. And now he saw he had reached a point he had often heard about, the sad, incredible region where the Indian forest had been cut down by the white destroyers and no place left for the Indian game to live. Here the desolate face of the earth had been exposed to dead brown weeds and stubble, lorded over by the lodges of the white people and the fat storehouses of their riches. Fort Pitt had been ugly, but it had still been Indian country. This, now, he knew, was the barbarous homeland of his white enemies.

He could feel them all around him. His moccasins tramped no longer soft mossy forest trails but a hard-rutted roadway. Curious wooden barriers ran alongside in a regular crooked fashion with spreading wooden horns at each angle. He was told they were meant to keep the white man's cattle from running free. The cattle stood tame and stolid as the soldiers passed, but the white people came running from their lodges to line the road. From the noise they made you might have thought the white army came from a great battle with loot and scalps instead of only children captives and without a shot having been fired.

Every hour the forest receded and the lodges of the whites grew more numerous. Late that afternoon they encamped near a white man's village. How could human beings, he wondered, live in such confinement! Here the whites had shut themselves up in prisons of gray stone and of red stone called brick, while the larger log houses had been covered over with smooth painted boards to give them the glittering ostentation and falseness so dear to the whites. Evidently their coming had been expected, for many people awaited them. Herds of saddled horses stood around. Men and women must have come a long way. Small crowds tried to storm the captives as soon as they arrived, but the soldiers held them off.

That evening the red-headed guard spoke to True Son in Delaware.

"Well, thank the Almighty I won't have to wet-nurse you much more. Your father's taking you over in the morning."

The boy gave no answer but the realization of who these people were swept over him. They were the captives' future masters, who could claim them and drag them off to a life of subjection in their own lodges. Among this company staring at him now was likely the one who pretended to be his own father.

The sun rose red and cold next morning. Through a frosty mist they were herded to the middle of the town where for a blocklike space no houses had been built, for what reason the boy did not know. It was early, but already the white people had gathered around fires trying to keep warm. Hardly had the captives arrived before they were stormed, taken by the hand, their faces sharply looked into, their scanty dress lifted apart for birthmarks, all the while their ears bombarded with questions that True Son could only in part understand. Then the Colonel and his staff put an end to it. They showed they had learned at least one thing from the Indians. They announced there would be no more confusion. All would be conducted according to rule and order.

Nothing of the scene that followed was missed by True Son—the swarming whites in cloaks and greatcoats, their heads scarved and hatted, and in their midst the sacrificial cluster of captives, mostly young, bareheaded, in simple Indian dress, with parts of their bodies exposed to the early winter wind. One unwilling young captive after another was brought forward, what was known about him or her announced, then a hearing given those who claimed relationship. Several times the crowd gave way to emotion, wiping eyes and blowing noses with a great fluttering of red, blue, white and other colored cloths. Even many of the white soldiers showed their feelings. Only the captives took it dry-eyed and restrained. True Son thought their Indian fathers and mothers would be proud of them.

At the end a very few were left unclaimed, including himself and two girls of twelve or fourteen years. The boy felt relief and hope creep over him. His white father didn't want him after all. He couldn't believe his good fortune. Now perhaps they would let him go back to his far off home along the Tuscarawas.

But presently above the murmurs of the departing crowd he heard the hoofbeat of horses in the strange town. Soon afterward a rider approached and the boy saw a small man on a sweated bay horse leading a saddled but riderless gray. In front of the Colonel and his staff, the rider dismounted. The Colonel shook hands with him and, smiling, led him over to where True Son and the unclaimed girls stood awaiting their fate. A chill ran up the boy's backbone. Surely he had nothing in common with this insignificant man with black boots, a face colorless as clay and a silly hat on his head. He came up anxiously and his very light blue eyes misted into the boy's face while the ashen hand he held out visibly trembled.

True Son stood rigid and unmoving.

"Put out your hand and shake his," Del Hardy ordered in Delaware.

Reluctantly the boy gave his hand. The man spoke a stammer of strange-sounding words.

"Your father welcomes you back," Del translated. "He thanks God you're safe and sound." When the boy's lips compressed, "Can't you say you're glad after all these years to see your own father?"

True Son's heart felt like a stone. How could this fantastic and inferior figure in a long fawn-colored garment like a woman's be possibly anything to him—this pallid creature who revealed his feelings in front of all! In the boy's mind came the picture of his Indian father. How differently he would have looked and acted. With what dignity and restraint he could conduct himself in any situation, in peace or war, in council or the hunt, with pipe or tomahawk, rifle or scalping knife. This weak and pale-skinned man was nothing beside him.

"He's not my father," he said.

Del Hardy made a face. When he repeated it to the white man, the latter seemed to recoil. The Colonel had been standing by following intently with his foreign eyes. Now he began to talk. The boy couldn't understand much of his mixed-up Yengwe tongue, but it looked and sounded like the Colonel was giving an order.

When they finished, the red-haired guard turned to the boy with a scowl.

"I thought I was rid of you," he spoke in Delaware. "Now I've got to go along and translate you to your own family."

The boy said nothing. His eyes gave a hard unwelcome. He knew instinctively that translating wasn't the chief reason for Del's going. No, the armed soldier was being sent along mostly to guard him, perhaps also to protect this slight presumptuous white man who claimed to be his father. Bitter disappointment came over the boy. Now he wouldn't be able to carry out his plan as soon as he had expected.

# vi

WHEN Del Hardy saw Fort Pitt through the trees, he threw his cap in the air. For weeks he had lived among savages in the wilderness. Now, thank God, he was laying eyes on a white man's settlement again. Sight of chimneys, of the certain slant of roofs with the British flag flying over them, stirred him deeply inside. These walls of mortared stone bespoke his own people. English or French, they had built to stay. This might be their farthest outpost now, but it wouldn't be long. He had heard a dozen soldiers say they were coming back to clear and settle the rich black land they had found along Yellow Creek beyond the Ohio.

His feet felt light as deer hooves climbing the mountains and jogging down the eastern slopes. He reckoned one of the pleasantest feelings a white man could have was, after tramping days in the everlasting forest, to come out on cleared land and look across open fields. Same way with a road. He had marched nigh onto three hundred miles on savage trails and traces, stumbling over roots and logs, slopping through runs and bogs. Now the hard firm ground of a cartway under foot lifted him up. His eye ran warmly over the good ruts, and the familiar zigzag of rail fences. Tame cattle in the fields stood quiet and decent as they passed. Here neither man nor beast had to be afraid of his shadow. The log barns and sheds on the land had an air of white man's industry and their houses of peace. From all of them young folk and old came to the road to rejoice as the army and its delivered captives passed.

That had been a day or two ago. Yesterday at Carlisle the freed white captives had been given back to the bosom of their families. You'd reckon by this time they'd learned to appreciate it. Yet, look at this Butler boy on ahead riding with his father, sullen as a young spider, making as though he didn't understand a word his father said. To watch him and listen to his Indian talk, you'd reckon English a bastard tongue and Delaware the only language fit to put in your mouth. You could see he still reckoned himself a savage and all those were black-guards and slavers who had anything to do with fetching him back to his own people. But then Indians were a strange lot. Del himself had lived neighbors to them as a boy. He knew their ways but never could he make them out.

Thank the Lord, he told himself, when they came to the home river. It would take his mind off the boy for a spell. The great stream flowed south from the mountains, a noble tide a mile wide. Just to let his eye roam over it gave him peace and wonder. The ferry pushing off from the far shore was a mark of civilization and the white race. To the north a squadron of islands swam like ships pointing down stream, and still farther north-ward were the majestic gaps of the Blue Mountains, one after the other, where the great river poured through.

It was to Del the greatest sight in his world. The nar-rower if deeper Ohio couldn't compare to it. And yet when he looked at the boy, he found him sitting his sad-dle unnoticing and unmoved. Not till they were on the ferry did he wake up to it. That was when his father called the river Susquehanna. Quickly, as if he had heard that name before, the boy lifted his head. His eyes took in the great stretch of water with the fields and houses on its far shore. Then he poured out bitter words in Delaware.

"What's he saying?" his father asked.

Del made a face.

"He says the Susquehanna and all the water flowing into it belongs to his Indian people. He says his Indian father lived on its banks to the north. The graves of his ancestors are beside it. He says he often heard his father tell how the river and graves were stolen from them by the white people."

Mr. Butler looked weary.

"Tell him we'll talk about that some other time. Tell him he's getting close to home now. If he'll look up at those hills across the river, he'll see Paxton township where he was born."

Even before he translated it, Del was sure the boy had understood. He gazed at the far bank with a sudden look of terror.

"Place of Peshtank white men?" he asked in thick, Indian English.

His father looked pleased. He put an affectionate hand on the boy's shoulder.

"That's right, son. Peshtank or Paxton. It's the same thing. We call them the Paxton boys. Many of them, I'm proud to say, are your own kin."

The boy looked as if a whiplash had hit him. He stared wildly up at the facing hills. The ferryman pushed by with his pole. The water curled around the flat bow of the scow. On the eastern bank, the sycamores and maples grew steadily nearer. Suddenly, before the boat touched shore, the boy kicked his moccasin heels into the sides of his horse and plunged with him into the shallow water. At once he was urging the gray with sharp Indian yells up the high steep bank. By the time Del and Mr. Butler reached the shore level, all they got was a glimpse of horse and boy vanishing into the northern forest.

"They'll stop him at Fort Hunter," the boy's father said.

But before reaching the fort, they came on the boy's horse standing riderless in the trail. Del jumped from the saddle and bent over the ground. In the thawed earth he could make out where the gray had shied at a white rag tied to a bush at a fork in the trail. In the ground were marks where the boy had landed. His tracks on foot were harder to follow, but Del ran down a path that led to the river. In a tangle of alders and sweetbrier he stopped and soon pulled out the kicking and biting boy. Mr. Butler had to help drag him back to his horse and lift him on the saddle. Then, with the gray firmly tethered between the two men, they rode back down the river trail.

They passed a mill, open fields, log and stone buildings. Their road climbed the rising hills. Now they could see rich, cleared farms with solid-looking houses and barns. The boy's father turned in to a lane lined with young walnuts. Ahead of them a barn with stone ends had the greatest space between them that Del Hardy thought he had ever seen in a building. Nearby was a limestone tenant house and, beyond the spring, a stone mansion house with a wide front door. As the riders approached, a boy and servant girl came out on the porch with a determined-looking woman beside them.

Del glanced at Mr. Butler. His face was uneasy. Likely he had looked forward to a time when his son would come back to him. But hardly had he counted on a homecoming like this. It would be an ordeal they would all have to go through.

The two men swung to the ground in front of the house, but the boy had to be ordered from the saddle. Del took him by the arm and led him to the porch steps.

"Your brother is home," the father said uncomfortably to the small boy standing there, then to True Son, "You never saw Gordie. He was born while you were away. But you ought to recollect your Aunt Kate."

The older boy stood silent in his Indian dress, ignoring all. The servant girl had started toward him. Now she stopped painfully, while Aunt Kate stared in frank disapproval and disbelief. Only the small boy seemed to see nothing unusual in the scene, gazing at his brother with open delight and admiration.

"Well, let's go in," the father said, clearing his throat, and they moved into the wide hall.

"Harry!" a lady's voice called eagerly from upstairs.

Mr. Butler and Aunt Kate exchanged glances.

"Harry!" the voice called again. "Aren't you bringing him up?"

The father gave a look as if there was no help for it.

"You better come along," he told the soldier significantly, then with the small boy running ahead and the aunt coming after, they urged True Son toward the stairs.

It wasn't easy to get him up. Plenty of times, Del knew, this boy must have shinned up cliffs and trees higher than this. But he eyed the stairs and bannister rail as an invention of the devil. For a while the guard figured this short distance from floor to floor might be the hardest part of their journey. Then Gordie, running ahead, turned the tide. He bounced up those steps so easy, looking around as he ran, that his brother shook off the hands that tried to help him. For a moment his eyes measured this white man's ladder, wide enough for two or three men abreast, the oaken treads shaven smooth as an axe handle and polished with a kind of beeswax. Then half crouching and taking two steps at a time, he climbed to the second-floor hall. It ran from one end of the house to the other, with doors branching off on both sides.

"This way, son," Mr. Butler said, and took him toward an open doorway where his small brother stood waiting.

The room they entered was large and sunny, with green-figured white walls. The broad flooring held much furniture, a red cherry bureau and washstand, a high polished chest of drawers, two or three small tables and twice as many chairs, a large bed with impressive posts, and by the window a couch on which a lady in a blue dressing-gown half sat and half lay. You could tell by the black hair and eyes and by the eager loving look she gave the boy that she was his mother. Just the same his father had to push him to the couch, and for all the notice he took of her, she might not have been there. Only when she pulled down his head and kissed him did he acknowledge her presence, stiffening painfully.

"Why, you look like an Indian, John!" she exclaimed. "You even walk like one. You've had a hard fate, but thank God your life was spared and you're home with us again. Are you happy?"

True Son had wrapped himself again in aloofness like a blanket. His mother turned with quick compassion.

"Doesn't he remember any English?"

"He understands a good deal, we think," his father said. "But not everything. We don't know how much he can talk it. So far he's only said a few words in English. Del has to talk to him in Indian."

"I'm sure he understands me," his mother declared. "I can tell by his eyes when I speak. You do understand me, don't you, John?"

The boy gave no response. She went on quickly, sympathetically.

"You've been away a long time, John. Your education has been arrested. You've had to live in heathen darkness and ignorance. Now you must make up for lost time. You're almost a young man. The first and most important thing to know is your native English tongue. We'll start right now. I am your mother, Myra Butler. This is your father, Harry Butler. Your brother is Gordon Butler. And you are John C. Butler. Now repeat it after me. John Cameron Butler."

The boy said nothing, only stood there impassively. Aunt Kate turned from the room as if she could stand no more.

"He don't know his own name. He don't even know when it's Sunday," Del heard her tell the servant girl on the stairs.

But back in her bedroom Mrs. Butler had far from given up. She might be an invalid, but you could tell she was the mistress of this house.

"I want you to repeat your name after me. Say John, John!" She seized his arm and shook it, then turned helplessly.

"Maybe he's deaf and dumb, Mamma!" little Gordie said.

That broke the strain for a moment and all smiled, all except the boy in Indian dress. Gradually his insistent, somber silence overtook the others. You could see Mrs. Butler come to a decision.

"Very well, John," she said, tightening her lips. "I see you are willful and stubborn as your Uncle Wilse. We will have to act accordingly. Your family and friends are coming to see you tomorrow and I won't have you standing up crude and ignorant as a savage in front of them. You'll have to stay in this room till you speak your own name."

You could see that the boy understood. Resentment crept into his dark face. He spoke rapidly in Delaware. Del had to translate it.

"He says his name is Lenni Quis. In English you'd call it Original Son or True Son."

Mrs. Butler heard him.

"But he's not with the Delawares any more. He's at home under our roof, and here he'll have to recognize his real name."

The boy regarded her with burning dark eyes so like her own.

"True Son my real name," he said in thick English, having trouble with the letter r. "My father and mother give me this name."

"He means his Indian father and mother," Del explained.

Mrs. Butler had flushed.

"Well, I think that will be enough today," she said. "He has spoken a few words in English at any rate."

She took from beside her on the couch some clothing she had been mending. A feeling of constriction crept over the boy when he saw they were a pair of light gray Yengwe pantaloons and a youth's yellow jacket. She went on. "When I heard you were coming home, I borrowed these from your cousin Alec. Now I'd like you to put them on and see how they fit you."

The boy made no effort to take them.

"Do you understand, John?" she repeated earnestly. "You're to put these on so we can see what you look like in civilized dress."

The boy stared with loathing at the pants and jacket. They were symbols of all the lies, thefts, and murders by the white man. Now he was asked to wear them. You might as well ask a deer to dress itself in the hide of its enemy, the wolf.

"Do you hear your mother?" Del said sharply and repeated the request in Delaware.

The boy still held back. How could he touch these things? Had there been small wood by the fireplace, he might have picked up the clothes with the end of a stick and carried them out, holding them as far from his body as possible. But there was no stick. Then Gordie took them for him.

"When you put these on, will you give me your Indian clothes, True Son?" he asked eagerly as they went from the room. "Then I can be an Indian."

The older boy did not say anything nor did he take off his Indian dress when they reached the room where Gordie took him, but for a moment a look of mutual respect and understanding passed between the two brothers.

"Shalehaha, a little boy, and Exundas, another boy. Tonquas was just a whip of a boy and Hyyenaes not much bigger. Koquaeunquas was the name of a little girl, Karendouah another girl, and Canukiesung the littlest girl of all. Not satisfied, the white barbarians scalped them. They did indecencies. They chopped off the hands of the men and squaws. They put guns in the mouth of one of our Conestogo cousins while he was yet speaking and blew his head to pieces."

Tonight True Son lay cold with hate just to remember. And now tomorrow some of these very men and their women were coming to welcome him. Their bloody hands would press his, calling him nephew and cousin. It gave him a feeling of abhorrence. Hardly could he bear even this white soldier, now in deep sleep beside him. At each snore, the boy began moving away from him, little by little, first one foot, then the other. It took a long time to work his way to the bed's edge and still longer to lower himself clear. Like a panther kit he crawled to the fireplace where embers still glowed. Here he stretched out. It was good to feel the hardness and coolness of the hearth-stone beneath him. A little air drifted under the door and across his face to be drawn up the chimney. He pulled his worn bearskin over him. Its familiar smell calmed him. It took him back to his father's cabin, blotting out the offensive scent of these white people. With the fur moving from his breath, he fell asleep.

At daylight he awoke with a jerk. He left the unpleasant jacket and pantaloons hanging from the peg in the wall of his room. At breakfast his white father and Aunt Kate looked disapprovingly at his Indian dress. He did not see his mother. Gordie told him that you didn't go into her room of a morning. When True Son came to midday dinner still in hunting frock and leggings, his

Aunt Kate was very stern. As he got up from his chair, she got up with him.

"Now I've had enough of this, Johnny," she said. "Your own kin are coming this afternoon to see you and we won't have you rigged out in your father's house like a naked and dirty savage. If you won't wash and dress, I'm coming up to wash and dress you my own self."

True Son didn't know every word she said but he understood enough so that cold horror shook him. This strong, ugly-looking white squaw looked as if she meant it. It reminded him of stories of squaws among the Ottawas who would run and catch a young man and undress him.

"I go look at clothes," he said with dignity in English.

"You're not just going to look at them!" she informed him sharply. "You're going to put them on. And you're going to wash yourself all over first or I'll do it for you."

He flinched. Gordie saw it with his quick eyes.

"I'll show him how, Aunt Kate!" he promised.

"Well, see that he does a good job or I will!" she warned. "Now come out in the kitchen, Johnny, and I'll give you some hot water to wash with."

He felt debased. He was an Indian male obeying a white squaw, made to carry with his own hands a bucket of steaming water up the stairs. That was woman's work back along the Tuscarawas. His only consolation was that his Indian father wasn't here to see. He thought he felt amusement on Del's face as he and Gordie instructed him to stand in a wooden tub. Then they showed him how to sop soap and water on his body from the white crockery basin.

When that was done, he could no longer postpone the crisis of the clothes. Gordie pointed out which was front and back. Revulsion grew as he drew the despised garments over his skin. Just to feel them about his flesh stung and bound him. Now he was thrice imprisoned—

first in this alien land, then in this Yengwe house and room, and last in this white boy's clothing. He turned away from the window as he saw the first visitors riding up the lane, none on foot, all proud with horses.

Gordie had to come for him twice before he would go down. He must remember what his real father had said—to conceal his true feelings from his enemies. First he had to present himself to his mother in her room and to the strange woman he found with her. Then slowly he went down the stairs. His father led him around the big parlor. A dozen people shook his hand, white uncles, aunts, and cousins. He couldn't tell one from the other. It was true what Cut Fingers back along the Tuscarawas had once said, that all white people looked alike. Only one stood out, a fattish boy who stared at his clothes, and True Son knew by his peculiar expression that this was Alec, whose jacket and pantaloons he wore.

At the end his father left him by his two uncles. Both sat back smoking. The lean and rangy one with loose skin on his jaw was his Uncle George Owens.

"Well, you can thank your lucky stars you're out of the clutches of those devils, Johnny," he said.

His Uncle Wilse, a powerful, heavy set man, swept the boy with slaty, less friendly eyes.

"He still looks like an Indian to me," he grunted, and True Son remembered what Gordie had told him, that his Uncle Wilse was a leader of the "Paxton boys." He tried to take no notice of either comment. His Uncle Wilse went on. "How long was he with those savages? Twelve years. Well, once an Indian, always an Indian. You can make an Indian out of a white man but you can never make a white man out of an Indian."

"Johnny is no Indian," the boy's father said uneasily. "He has the same white blood as you and I."

"It might have been white once," Uncle Wilse admitted. "But those savages brought it up red. It's the heathen notions they drill into him. Bad is good and good is bad. Stealing's a virtue. Lying's an art. Butchering and scalping white women and young ones is the master accomplishment."

The boy stood impassive, although he could feel the blood creeping up his neck and face. Uncle Wilse wached him darkly.

"Look at him now. Standing there cold-blooded as any redskin. I'll warrant he's hatching out deviltry in his heart." He looked at True Son and his slate eyes flamed with a dangerous smoky violet light that had only smoldered in them before. "Tell the truth, boy! Isn't that what you're doing right now?"

True Son gave no indication that he had heard.

"What's the matter with him?" Uncle Wilse growled. "Is he deaf or why doesn't he give his betters a civil answer?"

Del Hardy, who had been listening, moved up and repeated the questions to the boy in Delaware. Uncle Wilse interrupted.

"What kind of language is that?" And when he was told, "Can't he talk English, only that scrub Indian stuff? Well, if that's all he can talk, why doesn't he talk it?"

Del translated. The boy felt he could be honorably silent no longer. Holding himself erect as he could, he made an answer in Delaware.

"What did he say?" Uncle Wilse asked.

"He said Delaware isn't the scrub language you say. He says when Indians of different tribes meet, they talk to each other in Delaware. It's the master language of the Indians, and that's true. Most all tribes learn some of it so they can get along with other tribes."

Uncle Wilse had an expression of derision.

"What does it matter what gibberish Indians talk?"

True Son, listening closely, poured out a flood of words. Del translated it again.

"He says white people talk the Delaware language, too. He says we say tomahawk and wigwam and Susquehanna and other Delaware words. He says it's not a poor but a rich language. There's so many different ways of saying the same thing. You can always say just what you mean. He says, in English we say, God. But his Indian father, Cuyloga, told him there were more than twenty ways to say God in Delaware and each one means something different. There's Eliwuleck. That means, He that's above everything. There's Eluwitschanessik. That means, the strongest and most powerful One. Then there's Eluwilissit. That means, the One greatest in goodness—"

Uncle Wilse interrupted. His face was a picture.

"I can't stand that! You mean this heathen Indian, Cuyloga, who stole Johnny and claims to be his father, talks about God before he goes out and murders Christian men and women!"

At the reference to his Indian father, True Son felt his hackles rise. Suddenly a translator was too slow for him. He spoke to his Uncle Wilse direct, in English as best he could.

"Uncle. You talk about being Christian, but you murder the Conestogo!"

The heavy face flared.

"So you were lying to us when you said you couldn't talk English?"

"I no lie. I say nothing."

"No, but you tried to deceive us just the same, keeping quiet and making believe you didn't understand. That's an Indian trick and that's why the Conestogo got their just deserts at last. They pretended they were Christians so they could murder white people without being suspected or caught. If you tried to arrest them and put them to trial like anybody else, the Quakers took them to Philadelphia. They were only poor pagan Christians there. Rubbish! They were no more Christians than wolves!"

"I don't know," True Son said. "But they were people. Some good people, some bad maybe. But you were Christians. You had forty, fifty men. You had horses, knives, tomahawks, and rifles. You blow heads off of Indian men. You kill Indian women and young ones. Not one is left. You scalp. You chop. You cut off hands and try to cut off feet—"

Uncle Wilse's face was distorted. He got halfway to his feet.

"Yes, and that's the best thing that could have happened to them. They got what they deserved. We fixed the men so they wouldn't butcher any more of our people. And we fixed the squaws and young ones so they wouldn't breed any more murderers."

His shouting brought his son, Alec, to his side. The latter stood glaring at True Son.

"We give him my clothes, Papa," he said. "Then he stands there and insults us."

True Son flushed.

"I don't ask for clothes. I take clothes off and don't put them on again."

"Now that's enough!" Mr. Butler came to life. "Johnny, you can't talk this way to your elders. Tell your Uncle Wilse you're sorry."

The boy closed his lips tightly. His Uncle Wilse threw an angry, meaning glance at his brother-in-law.

"All I have to say, Harry, you better watch him. If he goes around siding against his own kin and neighbors, he's liable to get hurt."

For the first time since his initial greeting, the other uncle spoke.

"My boy, I want to tell you something. I'd hate to see you get the wrong impression of your family and especially of your father, Uncle Wilson and other Paxton men. In private life we're decent and respected citizens. We're members of Colonel Elder's church and subscribe to public benefits. But nobody can tell us anything about Indians. We've had too much experience. If a white man kills an Indian, he's called a murderer. He daren't be tried here where he'd surely be acquitted. No, he has to be taken to Philadelphia where he's convicted and hanged. But if an Indian kills a white man, he's just a poor pagan who doesn't know any better. He daren't be tried here either or he'd surely be convicted and hanged. So he's taken to Bucks County or Philadelphia where he's petted and sheltered and made a fuss of and never even goes to trial. That's the way it is between us and Indians, and why we've had to take the law in our own hands."

Uncle Wilse nodded grimly to the boy.

"I'll tell you something else. No Indian friends of yours better come to see you around here. If you expect that heathen abductor of yours, you better send him word to stay away."

A sudden fear struck the boy as he thought of the possible coming of his father. Bitter words poured out at his white uncle.

"Once a white man lived with Indians. He married Indian woman along the Muskingum. They had three young ones. All girls. One day white man makes mind he goes back to the people. He kills his squaw and three girls. He takes their scalps back to Philadelphia for scalp money. His name David Owens. Maybe you are his brother."

With the quickness of a giant cat, his Uncle Wilse moved to his feet and slapped the boy. The force of the blow almost knocked him down.

"No, I'm not his brother!" he shouted. "But I wish I was. He only did his duty to his country and his people. He believed in getting rid of vermin and so do I."

With great difficulty, True Son regained his posture. Now he stood straight and rigid. No more words, he told himself, would come from his mouth today. Around that mouth the white mark of his uncle's heavy hand still lay. At the owner of the hand his eyes burned with black, consuming hatred.

TRUE SON kept his word. That evening he pulled off the tainted clothes of his Cousin Alec and no one could induce him to let them touch his body again. Mornings he put on his Indian dress. When his father forbade him coming downstairs in it, he made a prison of his room. In a few days Peter Wormley, the Derry township tailor, came. He drew a painful face at the rude hunting-frock and leggings. What was he coming to, he complained, having to leave Captain Rebuck's fine broadcloth coat to dress a half-naked Indian boy!

Peter Wormley turned out two suits for the boy while he was there, one out of new cloth for Sunday, and one for weekdays from an old suit of his white father.

"Now take care of these!" he charged when he left. "Remember you're no young Injun running wild in the brush any more!"

Later Andy Goff, the shoemaker, arrived. The tailor's fitting and fussing had been trial enough, the clothes he made were ugly as Alec's. But the shoemaker was worse. The boots he pounded out were like half-hollowed logs. They gripped the boy's feet, wedged his toes, cramped his ankles. He felt that he stood in millstones. How could white men endure such things when

they might run light and free in moccasins? Next day
True Son went back to his Indian footgear. Then one
night when he lay half asleep, Aunt Kate came in and
took both pairs of moccasins. She carried off his Indian
dress, too, and now if the boy didn't want to languish
in bed, there was nothing for him to do but put on his
prisoner garb and clatter about in his hard leather boots.

It was done, he suspected, so he wouldn't run away,
for no man or boy could hope to get far through the
woods in such encumbrances. Already Del Hardy had
gone back to his regiment. At first True Son welcomed
his going, but once away, he missed him keenly. Of all
these white people he had known the guard the longest.
He was the only link to Half Arrow and his people along
the Tuscarawas. He had no one to speak Lenni Lenape
to any more.

And now all the odious and joyless life of the white
race, its incomprehensible customs and heavy ways, fell
on him like a plague. Every afternoon but the sixth and
seventh he must be a prisoner in his mother's bedroom
learning to read, making the tiresome Yengwe marks on
a slate. On the seventh morning he must sit, a captive between his father and Aunt Kate in what they called the
Great Spirit's lodge, with the strong scent of the white
people and their clothing about him. The whites were
very childish to believe that the God of the Whole Uni-
verse would stay in such a closed-up and stuffy place.
The Indians knew better—that the Great Spirit loved the
freedom of woods and streams where the air blew pure,
where the birds sang sweet, and nature made an endless
bower of praying-spots and worship-places.

Sometimes he felt the Great Spirit had utterly forgotten him in the white man's land. Then he would remember what Kringas back along the Tuscarawas had
told them. Kringas was old and rheumatic, a great-uncle
to Half Arrow. True Son could recall most every word.

"Nephews. Never think the Great Spirit forgets you. Some Indians think he favors the white people. They say the white people have their flocks of cattle to kill from when they are hungry. They have their barns filled with grain for their pots when they need it. The Indian has none of these. Nephews. Some think this is bad, but of truth it is good. It shows the Indian he is not supported by storehouses but by the Ruler of Heaven. Nephews. I have been young and now am very old. I have often been in want. It taught me that the Great Spirit suffers us Indians to be so for a purpose. It's to show us our dependence on Him who is the Father of us all and to let us know that if we do our part he will always supply us at just the right time. If we wait and are worthy, he will deliver the enemy into our hands."

Today True Son wondered if the Great Spirit had anything to do with his being sent out for a new bushel basket. Aunt Kate had sent Gordie along to show him where the basketmaker lived, but he suspected that Gordie was really the string to lead him back again. She need have no fear that he would run away on a day like today, for this was still the Month When Cold Makes the Trees Crack. The sun on the treeless white countryside blinded him, and his boots slipped in the snow as moccasins never would.

By and by they came to a little dark patch of woods near a run. In the woods was a log cabin. Blue smoke rose from the chimney. The door opened to their knock and a very old man with a brown wrinkled face stood there welcoming them. For a moment it was almost like being in the village at home. The ancient Negro basketmaker might have been an Indian. The cabin had a dirt floor like cabins along the Tuscarawas. The chinked logs and split white-oak baskets had such a smell of the Ohio woods that the boy was overwhelmed with homesickness.

He sat on the earth floor on a mat plaited from shavings, watching the wrinkled brown hands split the splints and weave them into a bushel basket.

"You're the Butler boy took by the Injuns?" the basketmaker said. "I heard about you. I was took myself when I was a little tyke. The Wyandottes got me down in Virginny. Before I was twenty a Pennsylvany captain got me out, and I been working for him ever since."

"You're a slave, Bejance," little Gordie said.

"I reckon I am, child," he agreed equably. "And so are you and your brother, though you don't know it yet. Now I know it too well. For nigh onto sixty years I been wantin' to go fishin' in the spring and summer, and huntin' fall and winter. But every spring and summer I had to work in the fields and every fall and winter in the woods. Now when I kain't work in the woods and fields no more, I kain't go out huntin' or fishin' neither. All I'm good for is sit on my bench and braid up hampers for the white folks."

"You're not free like us," Gordie declared.

"No. I'm never free from white folks," the Negro assented. "And neither are you and your brother. Every day they drop another fine strap around you. Little by little they buckle you up so you don't feel it too much at one time. Sooner or later they have you all hitched up, but you've got so used to it by that time you hardly know it. You eat with a fork and spoon. You sleep in a bed. You own a house and a piece of land and pays taxes. You hoe all day in the cornfield and toil and sweat a diggin' up stumps. Piece by piece you get broke in to livin' in a stall by night, and by day pullin' burdens that mean nothin' to the soul inside of you."

True Son felt a constriction in his chest.

"I'll never be a slave to the white people," he declared.

"Oh, you don't aim to, boy. Neither did I. I reckoned I was gettin' out of the woods. I was a goin' back home to fine folks and good livin'. I was gettin' back to good houses and barns and tools and wheat and barley fields, to clocks that told the time, and preachers that preached out of books and prayed your soul to heaven. Now I'm eighty-four years old near as I can make out, and the best I remember of my time is when I was a boy in the woods. I kin look back and see my whole life stretchin' like a cordstring behind me. And the brightest piece was when I ran free in the woods. It had a glory I ain't seen since."

True Son looked at him hungrily.

"Can you talk Lenape?"

"When I was young I could. Not Lenape but Wyandotte. I could rattle it off like I was born to it. But the Wyandottes and Lenni Lenape can't understand each other. Now the Shawanose and the Lenape kin."

"Not too good but they can make each other out," True Son said.

"That's what I say. The Shawanose and the Lenape kin make each other out. Once I could talk a little Lenape. All I recollect now is: *nitschu*, friend, and *auween kachev*, who are you, and *kella*, yes, and *matty*, no. I kain't even recollect much Wyandotte any more. Once when I was workin' up the river for Mr. McKee, a Wyandotte came through. I could understand everything he said to me, but it shamed me that I couldn't talk back to him."

"I was hoping you could talk Lenape with me." True Son was disappointed.

"No, they's only one left around here who can talk Lenape, or Delaware as they call it around here. That's old Corn Blade up on the Third Mountain, and I reckon he's a hundred years old."

"Where's the Third Mountain?"

"You know the Kittaniny Mountain? You kin see it from all over Paxton township. Well, that's what some call the First Mountain. The Second Mountain lays just beyond. Still farther north is a short mountain they sometimes call the Stony Mountain. It don't run out to the river. That's the Third Mountain. On top the Almighty left a pile of rocks like a church and on top of that a pulpit. Up in those rocks is where Corn Blade lives. How he keeps alive, nobody knows because he never comes down. He's afeard the Paxton Boys'll scalp him."

All the boy could think of when he got back to the house was the old Indian on the Third Mountain who could talk Lenape. Most of January, the month when the Ground Squirrels Begin to Run, he stood at the window looking north through the small panes. He couldn't see the Third but he could see the First Mountain. It rose from the fields dark brown and furry like the back of an immense beast. After a fresh snowfall the paths of the mountainside stood out clear. The deer paths were short. The wolves' paths were longer, crossing the mountain at dips in the ridges. Near the foot of the mountain a broad path ran level to the westward. It must be an Indian path, the boy told himself. In his mind he could see it running on and on, fording the Saosquahanaunk, crossing the mountains and rivers beyond till it reached the Tuscarawas where blue smoke rose from the dark weathered cabins, and quiet and peace lay over all.

Then it was February, the Month When the First Frog Croaks. One day the cold went and the rains came. Almost overnight the paths vanished, and the mountain turned from white to something dark, shaggy, and comfortingly wild. Just to look at it did something to the boy. He thought he could smell the forest as it smelled along the Tuscarawas after a rain, with the trees soaked black as ebony, and mosses on the bark and ground, green as splashes of paint. The ragged bark-flags of the

river birches would be flying redder than ever. The
buck's tail would lift white and unconstrained as he
sprang. The boy's heart filled with wild longing. He
could almost hear the sharp, fierce shout of his Indian
father's gun along the river and taste the aroma of
Kaak, the northern goose, roasting on the coals along
with his favorite cakes baked from Indian corn and
bean meal.

What he hungered for most was the sight of an Indian
face again—his father's, deep red, shaped like a hawk's,
used to riding the wind, always above the earth, letting
nothing small or of the village disturb him—his mother's,
fresh and brown yet indented with great arching cheek
wrinkles born of laughing and smiling, framing the
mouth, and across the forehead, horizontal lines like the
Indian sign of lightning, not from laughing but from war
and talk of war, from family cares and the strain of
labor—and his sisters' smooth young moon faces, not
pale and sickly like the faces of white girls, but the rich
blooming brown of the earth, their lively black eyes
looking out from under the blackest and heaviest of hair,
always with touches of some bright red cloth that set
them off and made them handsome. Even the ancient
face of Corn Blade, which must be no more than a
wrinkled brown mask, would do him good, the boy felt,
just to see it.

The Pawpawing Days passed. The Month of the Shad
came. The roots of grasses scented the thawing earth
and air. He could hardly wait. One day he took a loaf of
bread and piece of cold beef from the wooden safe
hanging in the cellar. Like a half-grown panther playing
at stalking its own den, he made his stealthy way to the
barn. Dock, the gray horse he had ridden from Carlisle,
stood long-haired in his stall. Bridle and saddle hung
from oaken pins. It did not take the boy long to ready

him, stowing meat and bread in the saddlebags. Then keeping the barn between him and the house, he led the horse toward freedom.

"True Son! Where are you going? Take me along!" Gordie called, running after.

He lifted the boy to the front of the saddle and climbed up behind. Once out of sight of the house, he turned Dock through the half-down bars to the open road. In time they passed a two-and-a-half-story house with a cooperage near by.

"That's Uncle Wilse's!" Gordie said. "And there's Cousin Alec. He's running in the shop to tell Uncle Wilse that we went by."

True Son didn't care. The earth was wide. The sky was the spread wings of a giant bluebird overhead. The sun shone warm. Dock splashed through runs that flowed full and wild. Down a long hill the road entered a dark green woods of pine and hemlock. Mysterious paths led through. A savage creek foamed in the hollow and delicious untamed scents rose from the ground and thicket.

He stopped the horse for a long time.

"True Son, what do you see? Do you hear something?" Gordie kept asking, but how could the older boy tell even his brother what he saw and heard! He let Dock stand in the woods cropping at twigs and buds. Why did the white race imprison itself in houses and barns when the life-giving forest stood all around? Kringas had spoken true. Perhaps the Ruler of Heaven and Earth had imprisoned him to make him value freedom when he got out. Never even along the Tuscarawas had he tasted such savor in the open trail, the sweet air, the green forest. Ahead lay the wide riches of the Saosquahanaunk, the shadowy water-gaps, the unseen valleys and streams, and then the Short Mountain with Corn Blade calling in good Lenape from the rocks on its summit.

They were coming in sight of the Narrows when the sound of hooves rose from behind them. Here in this deep, holy place where the river broke through the Kittaniny Mountains, True Son wished he could have been alone. He steeled himself against the strange men on horseback overtaking him. Then looking up with surprise he saw his father, Uncle Wilse and Neal, the farmer.

"So you were running away!" his father accused him.

"We were going to see Corn Blade," the boy said.

"Don't lie to your father!" Uncle Wilse threatened and True Son braced himself to be struck.

"Corn Blade is dead long ago," his father told him.

True Son said nothing. His Uncle Wilse reached into the bulging saddlebags.

"What's this?" he asked when he brought out the bread and cold meat.

"They were for Corn Blade," True Son said, but he saw that no one believed him.

"Did you know you were taking this stuff to Corn Blade?" Uncle Wilse put to Gordie who looked unhappy and kept still.

"So you lie and steal!" True Son's father reproached him.

"I told you what to expect, Harry," Uncle Wilse said.

"Well, we'll keep him under closer watch from now on," his father promised.

The boy tried to show no feeling. He kept the muscles of his face smooth as he had so often seen his Indian father do. The hardest thing, now that he had come so far, was to turn around and go back. He had lost all the precious beckoning things ahead. They had almost been his, the unseen valleys, the unforded streams, the untrodden forest and the great shaggy, unclimbed mountains that tried to push the white man, when he passed, into the river.

*ix*

IT was one of those unusually mild days that sometimes come to the lower Susquehanna in late March.
Outside, the sun shone. A song sparrow sang. The low
grass in the orchard already looked green. Two maples
in blossom stood red against the distant dark mountain.
You could smell the good, upturned earth where Neal and
a hired man were ploughing, with chickens and a robin
following the furrows.

But inside the big upstairs bedroom, Myra Butler had
her windows closed and the curtains drawn. She lay on
her couch in the welcome dimness with her eyes half
closed. She was thinking, as she had so much, of that
day in July eleven years ago. It was harvest time and
Harry was helping the cradlers. He had taken little
Johnny along. They were cutting wheat in the farthest
field that curved like a wide snaith into the timber sur-
rounding it on three sides. This timber and most of the
other woods that used to stand between here and the
Susquehanna was gone now, cut down and destroyed
in the Indian wars. But then it stood thick and heavy as
it had when the first settler came.

A hundred times she had heard the story and a hun-

56

dred times had she told it, how the savages had hid in the woods and watched the cradlers. How long they had been there no one knew, but with devilish cunning they waited till the harvesters were in the middle of the field far from their rifles stacked along the fence. Then they opened fire. Tom Galaugher was killed, and Mary Awl, who helped in the binding, was wounded. The other harvesters made their escape, all but little Johnny who had been left in the shade of a big hickory building a playhouse with shagbark. When the men came back with help and fresh arms, the boy was gone. They had kept the news from his mother as long as they could, but in the end they had to tell her the savages had her child. That was when Myra Butler had first taken to her bed.

Lying here this March morning with her eyes half closed, she thought she heard someone ride up to the house. Afterward there was the sound of feet on the stairs, a knock, and Kate's vigorous red face peered around the edge of the door.

"Parson Elder's come!" she said and came in. Swiftly she redded the room, drew back the curtains, combed her sister-in-law's hair and helped her into another gown.

Afterward a lean gray-haired man in black smallclothes, stockings, and slippers with fine silver buckles entered. He was much beloved in the two townships. His keen face seldom lost its gravity, and it didn't lose a shred of it now as he quietly crossed the room and pressed the invalid woman's hand.

"I saw Harry at the mill yesterday. He said you were poorly."

"It's nothing unusual, Parson," Myra Butler said. "But I'm always glad when you come."

"It's unusual enough, Parson!" Kate corrected bluntly.

Parson Elder glanced at one face, then the other. He was a leading citizen of the county, long pastor of the

Derry church, a colonel in the militia, a shrewd and successful farmer, and not easily affected by complaints and circumstances. Now he pulled a chair to the side of the couch and seated himself much as Dr. Childsley might have done.

"Tell me about it."

"There is nothing to tell," Myra Butler said. "As you know, I haven't been a well woman for more than eleven years."

"But she's worse lately," Kate put in. "And I'll tell you why, Parson. It's Johnny. You remember how often you prayed with her in this room that the Lord would restore him to her. Your prayers were righteous and the Lord answered them. Now you must do something about it, because you're the one responsible for getting him back."

The parson didn't look at Kate, only at Mrs. Butler.

"What's he done now?" he asked quietly.

The mother's lips closed tight, but Kate was quick to go on.

"You know how he tried to run off and take little Gordie along? It's lucky Harry and Wilse found him before he got away. Well, that's only a small part of it. He's a trial to all of us but Gordie. He's ungrateful. He won't own to his white skin. He still think's he's Indian. He says Indians don't have regular meal hours so he doesn't want to come to meals except when he's hungry. He shames us in front of the relations and neighbors. He won't join in our talk. He says we only know uninteresting things. He means we don't talk of savage things like beaver and panthers and bears and skins and scalps like the Indians. He believes Indians are sinless and perfect. He even believes it's right to lie and steal."

"I'm sure that's untrue!" Myra Butler declared quickly.

"Well, if it's untrue, then things here walk off by themselves," her sister-in-law answered tartly. "First it was one of your butcher knives. Then Harry's rifle went. Fortunately it wasn't his best. The brass part to the patch box is broken and Harry said he never liked it too much anyway because curly maple rusts the barrel. But it shoots to kill, and Harry says some powder and lead are gone, too. I've missed Indian meal. In fact, twice the bin was lower than I remembered."

"But you don't know definitely if anything was taken!" Myra Butler insisted.

"Not a hundred per cent. I only know somebody around here who doesn't like us. It don't matter about me but it galls me to see him treat his own mother and father like strangers. The Bible says, 'Honor thy father and mother that thy days may be long upon the land which the Lord thy God giveth thee.' But he only honors his false Indian father and mother and that's what's the matter with Myra."

"Kate—"

"It's true, Myra, and you know it. You've heard him talk almost every chance he gets of this Cuyloga and Queen Haga or whatever her name is. He may live in this house, but he's still a savage through and through. If he wasn't the image of his Grandfather Espy, I'd swear Colonel Bouquet made a mistake and sent us the offshoot of some squaw and no-account trader."

Myra Butler winced. The Reverend Elder saw it and sat back in his chair. He could afford to take his time and deliberate. It was a difficult subject.

"Perhaps I can talk to the boy for you," he said.

"I was hoping you would. I'll get Johnny for you," Kate told him and left the room.

Neither the parson nor Mrs. Butler heard the boy come in. One minute the two were talking together, and the next he stood inside the doorway, a lithe, dark-faced figure. In his jacket, pants and boots he might have been one of several well-to-do boys in the township. But on

second glance there was something different in the way
he held himself, an erectness, an intensity, an alien un-
manageable quality you could not lay your finger on.
Most boys brought in front of the formidable Parson
Elder were reluctant, some terrified, all uneasy. This
boy stood before him without fear or inferiority. Only
his eyes showed traces of unhappiness and concealed
hostility.

Before any of them could speak, Aunt Kate came
brushing through with pitcher and glasses on a brass
tray.

"You don't need to stand, Johnny," she told him.

He dropped down to sit on the floor, and the clergyman
noted the instant passage of pain across his mother's
face.

"There's a chair here by me, Johnny," he invited.

"I am used to sit on the floor," he answered. "Always
I sit on the ground outside. It is the lap of my mother,
the Earth."

Aunt Kate flashed a look at the parson. "You see!" it
said. The sweetish perfume of whiskey penetrated the
room as she poured the glasses. It was the custom of the
times, a full one to the clergyman, slightly lesser ones to
her sister-in-law and self, and one mixed with water to
Gordie who had followed her upstairs. Now she held up
the fifth glass already partly prepared with water.

"Johnny?" she asked but you could see she didn't expect him to take any.

The parson observed his refusal quietly.

"It would be more dutiful if you would join us,
Johnny," he said. "Your aunt invited you and it's well
to be obedient and of the same mind."

The boy's dark eyes met the minister's.

"I don't like," he said briefly.

"I'm not sure that all of us particularly like everything
we do on earth," the Reverend Elder commented slowly.

"However, there's such a thing among civilized people as putting off things of the flesh and showing charity and things of the spirit, especially in the home. If you practiced politeness and took a dram with us, you might feel more friendly towards God and man."

"My father told me why white people give rum to the Indian," the boy answered. "Get Indian drunk. Buy his furs cheap. Afterward Indian gets sober. Has no money, no furs, no nothing. Hates white people. Kills them some day. Now Aunt Kate gives rum to Gordie. You want give rum to me. You want make us hate you? You want make us kill you some day?"

Aunt Kate turned on him angrily.

"Now that's enough, Johnny," she threatened.

"I'll talk to him, Mrs. Stewart," the parson said. He turned to the boy. "John, what you say about some white traders is probably true. I've never seen it but I've heard of it and don't condone it. There are evil whites like everything else. But this fellowship between us isn't evil. It's just sociable. We are friends here together. We don't want to get anything out of you."

The boy's eyes showed disbelief.

"You want me your friend, you say. Maybe you want me to do like you. Want me baptize or pray to your God or believe things I be sorry for afterward."

There was an awkward silence. The parson flushed.

"I do want you to believe certain things that are good for your soul," he admitted. "Things that nearly all your white race believe in and practice. And I do want you to do some of the things I say. For instance, to treat your mother with kindness. Also not to lie, steal or swear."

"Indian only swear like he learns from the white man," the boy said. "My father says when he is a boy he hears white man say God damn. God damn when it rain and God damn if powder don't go off. So my father says God damn too. Then somebody tells him what God damn

mean—that the Great Spirit must burn it in hell fire forever. He is surprised. How could the Great Spirit bother
to burn in hell fire forever powder that don't go off? For
why would he burn rain when he made rain and sent it
on earth? After that my father don't swear. He tells me
never swear. It's the white man's lie."

"Well, I'm glad to hear such precepts from a pagan,"
the Reverend Elder said with dignity and just a little
sarcasm. "Did he also instruct you to treat your mother
and father with love and obedience?"

"Always I treat my father and mother with love and
obedience."

"He means his Indian father and mother," Aunt Kate
explained. "He won't believe that his Indian father ever
did anything bad and horrible like scalping white children and dashing their poor brains out against a tree."

"Is not true!" the boy cried, getting to his feet swiftly.
"But is true that white Peshtank men killed Conestogo
children, and Colonel Elder is captain of Peshtank men."

The shape of sarcasm rounding and modeling Parson
Elder's mouth slowly disintegrated. His face showed
pain.

"No one knows better than a preacher of the gospel
the dark unfathomable heart of man," he said sadly.
"Sometimes even the most exemplary Christians get out
of hand."

"Does good man like preacher get out of hand, too?"
the boy asked.

The parson gazed at him steadily.

"No, not often," he said. "I did what I could. As their
military leader, I ordered them to disperse and go home.
But they refused. Had I persisted, they would have killed
my favorite horse."

"Better your favorite horse dead than the favorite
young ones of the poor Indian," the boy asserted.

The Reverend Elder sat more powerful and self-restrained than Myra Butler had ever seen him.

"It's not only the white man who breaks the sixth commandment, Johnny," he said humbly. "Evil and ugly things have been committed against the will of God on both sides. Eight and nine years ago I never dared preach without a pair of loaded rifles in the pulpit. The men in my congregation kept their rifles standing by their pews. It was to discourage any of your red friends peeping in the window from trying to scalp us and our children. You say your foster Indian father never harmed a white child. It may be true. But I'm sorry to tell you that I know personally the authentic cases of many white children who were killed and mutilated by Indians. In one case the head was used as a football."

"Is not true!" the boy cried. "I see many scalp but no children scalp in our village. My father says men are cowards who fight children."

Aunt Kate had stepped up quickly to stop the boy, but the parson deterred her. His face was white. Despite that, he lifted his glass to his lips with great self-control. Sipping the whiskey coolly from time to time, he talked with strong earnestness to the boy of the brotherhood of man and the duties of Christians, red and white, to each other. He asked no questions that required answer, made no provocative statements and brooked no interruption. He closed with a long fervent prayer and then dismissed the boy.

When the latter was gone, the veteran parson wearily asked if he could have another glass.

"Living here near the frontier, we have our own particular trials and tribulations," he said. "This case of Johnny is not an easy one. But I don't think we should be too discouraged. It seems fairly natural under the circumstances for the boy to act this way. He's been in the hands of heathen for more than ten years. He's been virtually raised by them. Their character and philosophy was above the average savage, I'm glad to say, and you can be thankful for that. Just the same they were not white people, certainly not Christians, and you'll have to bear with their influence for a while. Ten years' teaching takes a long time to break down. You know what Proverbs says, 'Train up a child in the way he should go and when he is old he will not depart from it.' John has been brought up in the way he was not intended by his Maker to go, and it will take some effort to make him depart from it. But time is on our side."

"What can we do, Parson?" Myra Butler asked piteously.

"Just what you have been doing. Be grateful that God has given Johnny back while he's still a youth with a pliable mind. Teach him daily. Don't get discouraged. You see him every day and don't notice his improvement. But I see him only on the Sabbath or once in a while when I come here, and I can see a great change in him already. Despite himself, his English is better. Already he walks and gestures less like an Indian. You can't expect him to turn into a seraph or saint overnight. Don't push him too hard. Guide him little by little. Spring is here and soon he'll be working in the fields, getting up an appetite for the table. One of these days he'll notice some pretty and desirable girl. Pray God he takes a fancy to her. Then it won't be long till he's settled in our white way of life."

*x*

**H**ARRY BUTLER stood just inside the door. This was his son's room. It seemed curious that he hadn't been here since Johnny was back and probably wouldn't be now save for the boy's sickness. What that sickness was none of them exactly knew. Dr. Childsley had been here twice, the last time this very day when he had bled the boy's feet into a wicked-looking gallipot from his saddlebags.

But he wouldn't diagnose the trouble. The brusque Lancaster County doctor only looked grim, and muttered as he did the other time that the boy had lived too many years among the Indians, subject to their uncivilized fare, hardship and mode of life. Indians were liable to mysterious forest miasmas, he said, and at times they died like pigeons. Despite all curative knowledge, white physicians didn't know very much about these savage ailments. Cut them up, and the heathen had the same organs and muscles as civilized peoples, even to the exact shape and size of their bones. The blood they hemorrhaged was as rich and red as any white man's, but there were obscure primitive tendencies and susceptibilities in the aboriginal race, and they weren't helped by the superstition lurking in the dark and hidden recesses of the untutored mind. All he knew definitely was that the boy had some unknown fever, probably a result of his long unhappy captivity. This fever had remained unchanged now for nearly a week. It had refused to yield to powerful teas and powders. Sooner or later it would reach a crisis, and send the boy either into slow recovery or the grave.

The latter statement had shaken Harry Butler. He wished he could do something. The boy had been the victim of unhappy chance. If he hadn't taken him that day eleven years ago to play at the side of the wheat field, the Indians would never have got their heathen hands on him. Today he would be a different being, brought up on Christian precepts and the nourishing food and drink suitable to his race.

He wished he could talk to the boy, expressing these thoughts. It might release the burden long on his breast. Of course, he himself had really not been guilty, only the unwitting means that evil had used. Just the same if he bared his heart, it would relieve him and Johnny might bare his in return, expressing filial regret for his persistent and unhealthy passion for Indian ways and for his stubborn antagonism toward the decent thrifty ways of his white people. He might even confess his part in the disappearance of the curly maple rifle and ask forgiveness. In that event Harry Butler would completely pardon him and tell him that he meant to make him a present of it anyhow.

But for all the eager anxiety in the father's mind, the boy remained deaf to him, lying flat in bed without benefit of a bolster, the dark eyes in his flushed face gazing straight up at the ceiling. When his father spoke to him, he gave no sign except eventually to answer. But there was little warmth or affection in it, only a kind of brief and mechanical response. The older man might as well have been a stranger with no right to invade the boy's solitude and privacy.

It was curious how at such a time in the shadow of death all the belongings of the helpless victim affected a father to a degree he dared not speak of even to his wife. There from a row of wooden pins on the wall hung the still and mute clothing Johnny had worn in the sunlight of health—the weekday coat and pants made over from a suit the Reading tailor had cut for the father when he was still a young man—the boy's Sabbath clothes in which he attended divine service and listened to the word of God—also the miserable and pitiful Indian dress in which he had come home from captivity. Since the boy's illness, Aunt Kate had hurried to take it out of hiding and put it back, hoping it might console him and her own conscience as well.

In the end, the father left the bedside saddened and unrelieved. Going to a small room downstairs which had once been used as a cloak room but was now his office-room, he stood at the high desk and opened his heavy leather-bound account book. Hardly had he begun to set down the day's entries when he heard someone ride up to the house. There was a knock and Kate called him. When he got to the hall he found Parson Elder's son standing there in restrained excitement. He waited till Aunt Kate had gone.

"My father sent me over. There's Indians around and he wanted to warn you."

At once Mr. Butler took the younger man to his office-room and closed the door. Here he turned around, shocked.

"Indians! Why, we're at peace!"

"Maybe we are but they aren't," the other said. "One was shot tonight at Mehargue's pasture. He's lying down there now. Since Papa's head of the militia, Mr. Mehargue came right over."

"Any of our people attacked?"

"We don't know yet. They've seen only two of the savages so far. They stopped first down at the mill asking for the white boy that was taken from the Indians. The men at the mill sent them to Mr. Owens' cooper shop. At least, that's where the Indians went. My father thinks the men at the mill told them Mr. Owens was Johnny's uncle and that the Indians couldn't understand English very well and thought that Johnny lived there. But some think the men at the mill did it on purpose, for devilment. They know how much your brother-in-law hates Indians. But evidently Mr. Owens was very kind and hospitable. When one of the Indians asked for 'lum,' Mr. Owens gave him some. I believe the Indian had two or three mugs. Then he started boasting about himself and abusing the whites. There were some cronies with Mr. Owens and they said the Indians told degrading stories on the white people. Anyway about sundown the two Indians left. It was just getting dark when the Mehargues heard two shots. Some others heard them, too. When the Mehargues investigated, they found the Indian lying dead and scalped in their pasture. Mr. Mehargue said it looked like somebody had ambushed him from behind the trees because the Indian had been shot from the side and back. My father said he'd have him buried in the morning."

Harry Butler heard all this with a mixture of emotion. Troubles seldom came singly. Never had he known it to fail.

"Did your father say who he believed shot him?"

"He didn't say, sir." The younger man moved uneasily and declined to meet Mr. Butler's eyes.

"Did he say what happened to the other Indian?"

"Nobody's seen him since. If there were only two, my father think's he's back across the river by this time and still going. But you never know how many might be hiding in the mountain. My father thought you ought to hear right away. He said you'd likely want to keep it from Johnny. It might aggravate his sickness."

For a while after the rider had gone, Harry Butler stood thinking. If he told Kate, she would invariably tell Myra and that would upset her. Let her hover around for news. He would confide in no one for the present but keep his guns handy and loaded. When he heard Gordie trotting downstairs from his mother's room, he went back to his office. It was a relief at such a time to stand at his desk and straighten out his business affairs, to reckon up his accounts and property. When he opened the heavy brown-leathered book, the double pages with their solid lines of physical and financial items looked back at him, stable and reassuring. Presently the rough nib of his quill scratched roughly over the smooth blue and red lined surface of the thick page.

### May 31, 1765

*Sold this day holdover grain to one, Achmuty*

| 248 bus. | Wheat | at 4 | Shillings | a bus. |
|----------|-------|------|-----------|--------|
| 191  do  | Rey   | do 3 | do        | do     |
|  82  do  | Oats  | do 1 | do        | do     |

*Opened last Kag of Cydar. Very Potent*
*Sow Campbell sold me has Litter of 11*

He wished there might be more things to set down. Dealing with valid material things seldom failed to calm him. For a while he occupied himself counting the paper pound notes and silver shillings. The considerable sum steadied him. A pity his eldest son hadn't been raised to evaluate and enjoy the satisfaction and benefits of honest work, the solace and support of ready cash, and the remuneration and accumulation of active property.

FOR a long time True Son had felt the sickness coming on. The pain in his forehead refused to be wiped away. It was just his eyes, at first he told himself, and came from looking too hard for word from his Indian people. All winter his eyes had stared down the road and to the far hills across the river, straining for sight of a word-bringer from his people.

Now and then letters duly came for his white father and mother. His Indian father, he remembered, would get messages, too, mostly by messenger. His white parents' letters were quickly broken apart, read and thrown aside. His Indian father had more respect for words that somebody went to such trouble to send him. First the messenger was received and welcomed. He was made comfortable after his long journey and his wants supplied. Then when all was meet and ready, perhaps in the presence of others who had been called to hear, the message was given in words and dignity sometimes noble as an oration.

The boy knew it was a long way from the Tuscarawas to the banks of the Susquehanna, but word of mouth had been passed farther than that. There was always a way. Traders and hunters traveled back and forth. A message could even be sent by hand. The whites were not the only people able to make marks on wood or paper. He had seen his Indian father carve signs on the bark of a tree far in the woods, telling how he had shot a bear at this spot and that if the traveler left the path toward the west, he could find a spring of water where the elk or woods horse came to drink.

But winter passed and no word for him ever came that he knew about. The first green leaves of the Schka'ak lettuce scented the marshes. Birch buds stung the tongue, and the blossoms of the Tree of the Schwanammek lay in drifts on the mountainside like remnants of last year's snow. Hardly dare he look at them for homesickness. But it was the call of Memedhakemo, the turtle dove, that spoke to the very center of his being. Whenever he heard its note of lonely soliture, it carried him back on swift wings to the village on the Tuscarawas. It could almost be the same bird that used to sit on the hill of the High Spring and call in the early morning when the sun was breaking through the river mists. Then he could feel the bark town coming to life around him. Soon he and Half Arrow would be leaving for their day's freedom in the forest, chewing hunks of dried venison as they went. Where the river widened into a cattail swamp, their blood would race with the noisy talk of ducks and their fingers itch for the guns denied them. They complained of lost arrows shot across the water, but their fathers said if they had guns, they wouldn't get the bullets back either.

Other times they fished for Namespema, the rock fish, and waded in riffles for Machewachtey, the red-bellied terrapin. Often they didn't come back till Memedhakemo called again from the hill, and the village hung wreathed in woodsmoke flavored with the scent of roasting meat and of burning red-willow tobacco.

Oh, that was the life of young gods in the forest, and how could one think to live without it! All through the winter and early spring he told himself that when Hattawaniminschi, the dogwood, bloomed, he would have some word of greeting and encouragement from his Indian father, some message to keep up his courage and to say that the time of deliverance was near. But the fragile petals fell from the shad tree. Dogwood came into broad bloom. Now the leaves of Wipunquok, the gnarled and powerful white oak, hung tiny, pink and furry on massive branches. And still he heard nothing on the breeze that blew most every day from the Tuscarawas. It came over him that he was dead to his Indian people, his body buried, his grave neglected, his name forgotten as last autumn's leaves that had floated down the river never to be seen again.

The worst of it was that something had happened to his unquenchable Indian soul. When first they had taken him from the Lenni Lenape, he would have fought an army for the chance of returning. But now he had stayed in the insidious company of white people too long. Their milkwarm water had got into his blood. He had become tamed, submissive as a plough horse in the field. At first he had rebelled against the hoe. He had told his white father how once as a small boy the squaws had got him to help them hoe their corn. His Indian father had sternly reproved him. He was a manchild and should never dishonor himself with the labor of squaws.

But his white father could see no point in the story.

"We look at things differently here," he said.

A day or two later, old black Bejance came hobbling up the road on his two sticks. He gazed gravely over the fence at True Son and his hoe.

"They got the harness on you, Injun boy," he said. "The straps is buckled and the single-tree lugged."

The boy kept on down the row. That evening his white father spoke to him in the house.

"It wasn't so bad, was it, Johnny?" he smiled. "You did tolerable well for the first time."

His praise meant little to the boy, coming as it did from this man whose fondest place was his desk, his bald head bulging like a storehouse with useless figures of land, crops and money. He was still incomprehensible to his son, in dress and sex like a man and yet unable to rule his own squaw, but being ruled by her, obeying her slightest wish, paying others to do her work while she spent her life in her room like a sleek white rat in its cage, concerned mostly with newspapers, books and letters such as white rats liked to chew upon. Beside her, the memory of his Indian mother was like a spreading sugar maple providing them all with food and warmth, while beside this feeble white man at his desk, his Indian father had been an oak sheltering them from both the heat of the sun and the fury of the thunderbolt.

When they had put him to bed, his white mother, supported by his father and Aunt Kate, came to his room to read to him from the black book she said God had given the white people. Later the white medicine man appeared, smelling of horses, practicing the white man's superstition of bleeding the feet and purging with powders. The boy let them do with him as they would. In his heart he felt there was no use. Let the whites tie the Indian, imprison him, surround him with guards night and day, still they couldn't hold him. There was provided for him a way of escape. He need not walk or run in it, only yield to the inward voice telling him what to do, let himself sink, permit the light of day to close over him, and the prison cell would be left empty above him.

He was dimly aware this evening that something out of

the ordinary had happened. He heard the gallop of a horse. Later the sounds of commotion rose from the back porch.

"Go 'way! Vamoose!" he heard Aunt Kate call. She sounded very cross.

Soon Gordie came to bed in excitement. He said Aunt Kate had seen an Indian looking through the kitchen window. The Indian had run like a coward when she went to the door with her broom.

True Son lay very still, letting the words sink into his mind. So one of his people was near! Perhaps the long-awaited message had come. At the thought, a lump long hard and dried up inside of him melted. A door he had never seen opened in his breast and the first trickle of life-giving substance came through. Motionless he waited till Gordie slept in bed beside him. Then he sat up.

He felt very weak but stronger than he expected. The room stretched about him, faintly light with the night. After a while he put his feet to the floor. His Indian dress, he saw, hung beside his white clothes from a peg. He had not been forgotten by the Great Spirit. Everything had been provided. From time to time he rested on the chair from his small exertions. At last he climbed out of the open window, lowering himself till his moccasins touched the roof tiles of the low kitchen wing. Then he let himself fall and slide like a crumpled ball of spider down to the lap of his mother, the Earth.

His aunt, the Night, with her cool hands, received him. His brother-in-law, the West Wind, with his clear breath revived him. His very old uncle, the Moon, shone down upon him. When from the shadow of the barn he looked back, the big white stone house stood like some monster created by the white people, staring after him with one hostile yellow lamplit eye. It was good to look the other way in the soft, endless Indian moonlight, which was never shut up in houses, never having to be bought in white man's posts or lighted in a pot, but free to all the earth and its creatures.

Across the big field of tiny corn, he stopped where the fence row of sassafras trees made a shadow in which he could hide. There was no sound save of distant hounds. Into the stillness he threw out the regular spaced notes of Chingokhos, the big-eared owl. Utter quiet followed as if even the dogs listened. After an interval he called again, telling a listener what white men would never notice that, although owls called from near and far in flight, his own calls came from the same place. Still there was silence. He called the third time, and now he added the unmistakable rasping whoo-haw of Schachach-gokhos, the barred owl, on the end.

This time an answer rang so close from across the fence row in front of him that he almost jumped. He guessed that all the time the answerer had been moving noiselessly toward him.

"*Auween khackev?* Who are you?" he called very low in Delaware.

"*Lenape n'hackey.* I am Indian," a guarded voice he was sure he had heard before, answered. "*Auween khackev?*"

"I am Lenape, too. Come out and let me look on you."

But the unseen speaker in the fence row did not stir. True Son moved closer and still he could see nothing.

"*Lenni Lenape ta koom?* Delaware, where do you come from?" he asked.

"*Otenink Tuscarawas noom.* From the town on the Tuscarawas," the answer came, and now True Son was sure of the voice. A surge of joy lightened him.

"Half Arrow! *Ili klehelechc!* Do you still breathe!" he cried. A bush detached itself from another bush and in the dim light the two boys rushed to each other. They embraced and cried out, gripping each other's arms. Half Arrow's fingers were iron.

"Cousin! I didn't know you. Your voice was like a Yengwe's trying to be Indian."

"*Ehih!* Am I that bad?" True Son muttered.

"But now with me you will soon talk better!" Half Arrow promised.

"I hope. Let us go to the house."

But Half Arrow drew back.

"Cousin. It's better not to. I don't dare trust the white people. Already I am chased off by your white mother. She called bad names. She would not like to see me again."

"It wasn't my white mother, only Piwitak, the aunt. You mustn't let the rudeness of white people affect you. They are young and haven't learned yet the hospitality of our Indian houses. If I ask them to, they will feed you."

"No, I am not hungry. I ate yesterday with Little Crane."

"Little Crane!" True Son said the name with delight. "Does he still breathe! Is he already a papa and how is his feeling for his young white squaw?"

"All the way from Tuscarawas he talked of her. But she is still two days' journey off."

"I hope he's not gone to her so I can still see him," True Son said.

"No, he's not gone, and you can see him," Half Arrow promised but his voice sounded strange.

On the way, one ahead of the other, True Son plied questions, and Half Arrow answered. It was like medicine to hear the familiar boyhood tongue with the good whistling sound of the Indian consonant which white people did not have, and to speak without having to set his lips or tongue for the foolish Yengwe V and D which the Lenape did not need. All the way his spirits lifted so that he didn't notice where they were going. Then suddenly he saw they approached Mehargue's pasture and that Half Arrow had stopped speaking and was moving with slowness and caution.

"Why do you drag?" True Son asked. "If you whistle like the crane, then he will answer unless now since he is a papa he has become deaf."

"He is deaf enough," Half Arrow answered, moving from tree to tree where he paused and listened as if not for a friend but an enemy. At last he halted.

"I said I would bring you to him. Here he is," he said in a dull voice.

"Where? I see no one, unless he's a tree."

"He is something like a tree. Do you see him now?"

True Son strained his eyes through the shadows. All the trees he saw bore limbs and leaves. Then slowly he became conscious of a dark mark on the ground. He had taken it for one of the short logs of the white people.

"That which lies like a cut tree isn't he?" he asked.

For answer Half Arrow ran and knelt at the dark mound.

"Ai, for the Lenni Lenape!" he cried and gave a long Indian moan.

True Son came slowly closer. Even in the dimness he could make out the design of the familiar match coat Little Crane had worn last fall. It had been spread like a blanket, but the body beneath it neither moved nor spoke. True Son stared in rigid disbelief.

"Cousin. It was not sickness that brought him down?"

"No, it was not the sickness."

"It was not the Frightener that white people call the rattlesnake?"

"No, it was not the Frightener."

As True Son bent over the body, he felt a terrible hate for the ones who had done this. Could this hard and dried blood on the match coat be the life fluid that only

a few hours ago had flowed through Little Crane's veins
and had brought him all this distance but now could
carry him no farther?

"Cousin. Who did this evil thing?"

"The shots came from behind. When I looked the
butchers were over there behind the trees."

"Cousin. Where were you and what did you do that
men would shoot after you in peace?"

"We did nothing and stopped at only two places. The
first place we asked for you. They sent us to the second
place. It was your white uncle who has men making kegs
and barrels. But you were not there."

"Did you or Little Crane say anything to make him
cross?"

"Cousin. Before we went in, Little Crane said we must
remember we are guests of the white man. We must be
polite. If you look at the skin of a white man, he said,
you can see how thin and weak it is. Even such a small
thing as words will bruise and cut it open. So we must
not remind the white man what he knows very well, that
his land rightfully belongs to the Indian from whom he
stole it. No, we must be happy and tell happy stories. So
when we went in, Little Crane was happy and told happy
stories."

"Do you remember any of these happy stories?"

"Two I remember. They were very funny. Once some
Mingue stopped with a white missionary overnight and
put their horses in his grass field. The missionary chased
their horses out of the field. He said he intended mow-
ing the grass for hay. The Mingue said, Friend, the field
is on Indian land. Then how is it your grass? Oh, yes it
is my grass, the missionary said. I fenced it in. But who
grew the grass, you or the Great Spirit? the Mingue
asked. The Great Spirit grew it, the missionary had to say.
Then our horses have a right in it, the Mingue said, because we are the Great Spirit's children. Little Crane

said you had to laugh at the missionary's face when the Mingue put their horses back in and ate up the grass. He was not a real Quekel but wore a big hat like the Quekel. Little Crane himself had to laugh when he told it. Is there anything so funny, he asked the white men, as a man thinking he owns Indian land if he fences it in?"

True Son stirred uneasily.

"Cousin. You said there was another story."

"That was very happy, too. It was about a Shawano who owed the white man he gave his trade to. The trader said he must pay up. He daren't even wait for winter when his pelts of the beaver and fisher fox would be prime. The Shawano asked if cattle hides taken in the summer time would be good in trade, and the trader said, yes he would salt them down. So the Shawano settled his debt with cattle hides, and not till the Shawano was gone did the trader find out the hides were from his own cattle. Cousin, it was a very happy story. I heard it once at home in the village and the squaws had to hold their sides with laughing."

True Son stirred again. This was the bold, full-flavored Indian humor he had longed for. But he couldn't laugh tonight.

"Did the men at my white uncle's laugh?" he asked.

"Cousin. They didn't laugh. When we left your white uncle, Little Crane said to me, the white men are beyond Indian understanding. No matter how happy we talk, they won't laugh with us."

Half Arrow lifted the blanket from the body and True Son saw with horror that his friend had been scalped. His cold savage rage rose and consumed him.

"First let us give Little Crane rest," he said. "Then we go to my white uncle and ask him who is the murderer."

With Half Arrow's knife and tomahawk, they cut out a shallow grave. On the mound they laid branches from the bushes in Indian fashion. Weak with exertion and covered with sweat, True Son led the way to the two-story house with the cooperage beside it. A shed was piled with hoop poles and stacked with new barrels and kegs shining white as skeletons in the moonlight.

The cooper shop was dark but light still showed in the house. True Son knocked and the short thick form of Uncle Wilse came to the door. At the sight of him, the boy's hate for this man who had slapped him rose and his voice with it.

"Where's Little Crane?" he accused shrilly.

His uncle stood stocky and untouched, peering out at him.

"If that's one of those Indians that was here," he said, "he's where he won't do any more mischief." He suddenly recognized the caller. "So it's you, boy! I thought you were sick and going to die. Does your father know where you're at? I reckon I better keep you till I tell him."

His quick stubby fingers shot out and caught hold of the boy. True Son struggled to free himself but the powerful hairy hands easily held him fast.

"*Itschemil!* Help me!" he gasped and, with a rush, Half Arrow came out of the shadows.

He struck with such force that the unprepared man went down. Even so, he was more than a match for the two boys. Half rising, he threw Half Arrow back with one hand while he choked the kicking and writhing True Son into submission with the other. Things were going black before the boy's eyes when he saw Half Arrow return with a rush. The good Indian hate was on his face and a hoop pole swinging in his hands. It struck the heavy head of the white man who grunted and fell forward. True Son felt his own breath and sight come back as the death grip on his throat relaxed.

Quickly Half Arrow threw down the pole and pulled out his knife.

"*Pennaul* Now watch me cut out his black heart!"

"*Matta.* No." True Son said with regret. "He calls himself my uncle."

"Then let us skin him like a beast."

"*Tah.* It takes too long."

"Well, anyhow, we will take his hair like he took Little Crane's. *Lachil* Quick!" Half Arrow gave him his tomahawk and the two set to work together, one cutting, one hacking. At the pain, the heavy white man stirred, groaning loudly, and before they had got very far, steps sounded on the floor above them. One of the cooper hands who boarded with his master appeared suddenly on the stairs. With an exclamation of dismay, he hurried back.

"When we are done with this one, we will scalp him too," Half Arrow declared confidently.

"No, he goes for his gun," True Son said. "*Kshamehellatan!* Let us run together."

Giving up their trophy with regret, the two youths faded into the night. True Son led the shortest way across fields to his father's farm. The big stone house, the small house and barn all stood dark.

In the pitch blackness of the barn floor, he felt his whispering way to a mow where he burrowed deep under the hay. From here he brought mysterious articles that out in the moonlight became a bag of meal, a tow wallet of lead balls, a knife, a horn heavy with powder, his old bearskin and a long rifle with the brass patch broken off.

"*Jul*" Half Arrow exclaimed with delight at the sight of the rifle. He took it admiringly in his hands. "What a pity we did not have this at your white uncle's. Then we could have got his scalp and the other white devil's too. Now we could dance around the scalps. We could spit on them and sing revenge for the murder of our brother."

"Listen!" True Son said. "Somebody goes for help against us."

They could hear plainly the gallop of a horse across the valley. Most of their way to the wall of the First Mountain the sounds followed them, of other horses pounding the roads, raising the alarm in Paxton township.

## xii

WHEN True Son woke, he didn't know at first where he was. All he could remember was his sickbed in the house of his white father. He had expected he would die. Could this be the bright land of death, where all was made right? He remembered he had been weak. Now he felt strong. He had been bound. Now he was free. He had lain for days sealed in by the white man's plaster. Now he lay in the infinite open with green leaves moving over him and fresh air blowing on his face. His father, the Sun, had already risen. Around him his sisters, the Birds, sang. His brother, the Black Squirrel, coughed at him. His mother, the Earth, bore him up on her breast, while all his small cousins that stood or ran upon the earth spoke their scents to him—the Fox and the Pine, the Hemlock that men used for tanning, the Medicine Plants, the aromatic Spice Bush that bloomed in the spring and the Hazel that bloomed in the fall.

Then he thought he couldn't be dead, for somebody snored beside him. He turned his head and found Half Arrow's coal black hair close to his face. Seeing that coarse hair sent the love for his cousin through him. He had come all the long way across mountains and rivers through a dangerous land just to reach his side. Through the night they had lain like brothers, close as chestnuts in a burr for warmth. His old worn bearskin below served them both, Half Arrow's blanket above.

And now he remembered what had happened last night and that where they camped was the top of the Kittaniny Mountain he had watched so long from his white father's farm. Joy rose in him at the thought that he couldn't go back, for, if he did, they would surely put him and Half Arrow in irons. And if this white uncle died, they would hang them by the neck in the barbarous custom of white people. Even if freed, the friends of his white uncle would never let him live. He and Half Arrow would be ambushed and scalped, their hands cut off like the young boys, Shalekaha, Exundas and Tonquas of the Conestogo.

"Cousin!" he breathed, and he knew by the quickly halted breath that Half Arrow was awake. "We waste daylight. Let's go before the white men catch us."

Half Arrow sat up instantly.

"Where are the white devils?" he demanded.

"They're not here yet but they soon will be."

"*Elke!* That's good. Then I can sleep again."

"No, we have many hundred miles to go."

Half Arrow gave him a look. He jumped to his feet like a deer.

"Cousin. You mean I don't go back all that long way alone?"

At True Son's answer, he broke off two branches of hemlock. Holding one in each hand above his head, he began to dance around his cousin chanting foolish Lenape words of triumph.

"*Sehe!* Not so loud," True Son cautioned. "They will hear you down in the valley."

"They are too deaf," Half Arrow boasted. He stopped, as if with contempt for the whites, to make his water far over a log. "They can hear only the war whoop and the money rattle." He finished with alacrity and a flourish of drops. "Maybe we better go just the same," he said and started to scoop up his carrying share of the belongings.

Down the north side of the mountain, they avoided white hunters' paths. Their moccasins sought to disturb no leaves or sticks, stepping from stone to stone. Now and then both boys stopped to listen. At the first run they clapped palms of meal from the sack to their mouths, washing it down with water in Indian fashion.

Half Arrow smacked his lips.

"Now I can go till evening," he promised.

Under cover of trees and brush they crept among the next valley's clearing. They climbed the second mountain, fording the second creek when they came down on the other side. Always they avoided the river trail. The third mountain they did not have to climb. As the old basket-maker said, it stood drawn back from its companions like a noble chief aloof from his fellows. True Son pointed out to Half Arrow the pile of rocks at the top where Bejance said the old Lenni Lanape lived. But they had no time to look for him now.

Cutting northwest, they crossed the trail, forded the third stream at a cliff red with rock flowers and pressed on toward the point of the fourth mountain where the great river broke through. Here True Son's strength gave out, and the rest of the day they lay in the woods. Twice they heard parties of white men crossing the valley, some on horseback, calling to each other and talking noisily. Once the sound of a rifle echoed from mountain to mountain.

For a while Half Arrow was gone to spy. He said on his return he had seen half the world from a tree on the mountain. A large creek flowed into the other side of the river, and a ford of rocks led to it. Before daylight both boys were at the river's edge, wet by the heavy mist,

trying to peer across. At the first streaks of daylight they
set their feet in the water. They found the rocks wet and
slippery, tilting up sharply from the foundations of the
mountain that once must had stood here. It was a hard
crossing. Where the rocks failed, the boys had to wade.
When the friendly screen of mist dissolved, most of the
wide river lay behind.

True Son shivered with wet and cold. Since day before
yesterday he had tasted no food save raw meal and water.
And yet now as he climbed out on the western Saosquahanaunk shore, he felt around him a golden and purple
brightness as if the sun had risen over the mountains behind him. He had escaped from his Peshtank prison at
last. The very trees of the forest looked different over
here. The unknown creek from the west flowed brown
and primitive as a naked Lenni Lenape.

His only shaft of regret was leaving Gordie. He could
see him in his mind now, lying alone on their wide bed,
a chattering squirrel by day, a bed-warming stone by
night, only a little minny of a fellow waiting for his Indian brother who would never return. For a long count
while Half Arrow watched silently, True Son stood on
the point of land between the two streams, gazing down
the broad watery road through the mountain gaps that
opened like majestic gates toward his white father's
house.

"You sorry! You don't want to go?" Half Arrow asked.

"Cousin. Nothing holds me now," True Son told him.
"Cousin. I leave a small white brother. Out along the
Tuscarawas I have only sisters. Cousin. From today on,
you must be my brother."

For a long time they traveled blind, for there were
high cliffs, thick woods, and no paths. Then suddenly
they broke out on a narrow well-worn trail coming over
the hills to meet the small river. Their feet took to it like

wings. The very breath of the path was Indian. It dipped through the dim pungency of pine groves where hardly would you know the season, and it broke out into the bright new greenness of the hardwoods where even the blind could tell that this was the Month When the Deer Turns Red.

Always the endless Indian forest stood above them. When it thinned, there were the crimson Indian Hearts that white people call strawberry and the purple swords of Indian raspberries. Fish leaped from the creek and pheasants made thunder through the trees. Not often was Half Arrow silent. He pointed out the meaning of signs and droppings as if his companion so long among the whites had forgotten. Oh, never, True Son told himself, would he forget this path, this westward, ever westward path, deep in their Indian forest, with his cousin tramping before him, pointing and talking, giving thanks to every spring that ran across their path, for hadn't this water they cupped to drink lain deep in the dark caverns of their mother, the Earth, to be brought out just for their refreshment as they passed!

Only once, when the forest gave way to the cleared fields of a colony of whites, did Half Arrow's good humor leave him.

"*Lennau!* Look at them. Cutters down of the Indian forest! Stealers of the Indian land. Let's give them a present of Indian lead. In return we'll take presents for our Indian brothers."

But all the time he talked, Half Arrow kept to the path, berating the thieving whites, regretting there were only two against so many and that he and True Son would have so far to carry booty.

"Ah well, lead is scarce," he said. "We will let them breathe this time. But didn't we fix that old *schwannack* of your white uncle who scalped Little Crane! He won't

forget us in a hurry. If he lives, he is rubbing his head
right now. *Yuh allacque!* What a pity we didn't finish
him when we had a chance."

It made them a little uneasy when their path joined a
deeper and wider path. It came pouring down through a
mountain gap. You could see that white men and their
horses had trod this path. But its makers must have been
Indian, for it looked as if long before white men came it
had been here. His own people, the Lenni Lenape, must
have traveled it, the Shawanose, the Nanticokes, the
Ganawese and Saosquahanaunks. Even distant nations
had helped to pack it, the Sankhicani or Gunlock people
that the whites call Mohawks; the W'Tassone or stone-
pipe makers, called the Oneidas; the Onandagos or
hilltop people; the Cuyugas or lake dwellers; the Mea-
chachtinny or mountaineers that the whites call the
Senecas; and the Tuscarawas, called by all Tuscarawas,
for the word rolls easy from the tongue so that wherever
they go mountains, streams and valleys are called after
them. All these latter were the Mengue which the whites
called the Mingoes or Six Nations, and the French, the
Iroquois. But many others must have tramped this path,
too, the Cherokees and Catawbas, the Kanahawas who
should be called the Canai; the Mohican or River Indians, the Wyandottes that the French call Huron; and
perhaps even the far eastern Abenakis who are brothers
of the Lenni Lenape and speak a dialect of the Lenni
Lenape tongue.

And yet for all those red peoples and nations who had
trod it, not an Indian did they see that day. So far had
the whites driven them from this country. Only twice did
the two boys have to lie in the woods while parties
passed, once when three white men came suddenly on
foot, and another time when a train of nineteen pack
horses slid down the mountain. Armed traders guarded
them. Every bale of pelts on the horses' backs was a

message from home. Surely, Half Arrow chattered, they
were on the right track, for those pelts could only have
come from Indian country, perhaps even from the Forks
of the Muskingum and their own village on the Tuscarawas.

That night they lay on the western side of a mountain.
Now not a river alone but a great wall was between
them and the Peshtank country. Next morning their legs
put a still bigger mountain behind them, and now they
went on the path with less caution. Freely they baked
cakes of Indian meal over their fire and roasted game
shot by the striped rifle. Oh, they hid quickly enough
from any armed men they saw who might take a fancy
to their hair. But the deeper they went in the forest, the
nearer they felt to home. They tramped a deep, long
valley; saw sleeping cabins for white traders; drank from
a spring around which you could see great numbers of
red and white men had once camped; passed the Shades
of Death where two mountains stood close and dark with
ancient pines and hemlocks between.

At a fork in the trail, they took the north branch. Always they kept apart from the Bedford road to the south
where the Peshtank men might seek them. Three times
in one day the trail forded the same river. They passed
an old Indian town and traversed the longest Narrows
either of them had ever seen, stopping to see a curious
stone as high as three men and only a few inches square,
pointing to the heaven.

"I have heard of this stone," Half Arrow said. "Now
if those that spoke knew the truth, only one mountain
stands between us and the Tuscarawas."

They came on that mountain next day. Their breath
grew short on the way up, for this was the tallest hill of
all. But when they reached the top they found this was
no mountain like the others, a steep way up, a steep way
down and a sharp summit. The top of this mountain was

very wide, stretching on and on, a high country with immense timber. They passed a few cleared fields, old Indian cabins, some beaver dams and a deer lick many miles long. So they kept on for two days until they met a river flowing strong and deep through the forest.

An Indian track went up and down, and on the bank stood the log buildings of a trader. A few Indians loafed in front. Through the open door the eyes of the two boys caught the glitter of much goods. Once the trader himself came out to take oars from one of the smaller of two dugouts bobbing at the landing. The two boys did not venture close but sat on the roots of a buttonwood at the edge of the water.

"I have heard of this river," Half Arrow told. "They call it the Alleghi Sipu. From here, it is said, fish can swim to the Forks of the Muskingum."

"Maybe it is so," True Son agreed, "but we are not fish."

"No, but if a fish can swim, a boat can float, and the Father of Heaven has already provided two boats at the landing."

True Son considered.

"I see the two boats. But they belong to the trader."

"Cousin. You have been too long among the whites. They have corrupted you in your thinking. You have believed their false claims that justify their plunder and pillage. Now, all we Indians know it is not stealing to take back from the whites what they took from us. Cousin. What have they taken from us? Land, woods, game, streams, fish and our happiness. Cousin. Look at the white trader's fine house and all his possessions. Think how much he must have stolen from the poor Indians who trade with him."

"He is only half white and half Indian, I think."

"Then we will take only half of his boats," Half Arrow answered brightly. "I think we will choose the larger, for there are two of us and only one of him. He will thank us tomorrow morning for leaving him any boat at all."

"The trader has dogs," True Son reminded him. "The dogs won't thank us for coming to the landing at night."

"Only a white man would go up on a trader's landing at night," Half Arrow said. "First my father would cut a dry wind-fallen pole. Then he would float down the river like two sticks of wood in the night. His knife would cut the boat's thong. The dugout would float willingly downstream with him till out of scent and hearing. Then my father would climb in. I wonder that the trader never lost these fine dugouts before."

Later True Son went down the river trail alone. He carried the packs, the almost-empty sack of meal, the powder horn and the rifle. Far out of sight of the post, he cut a pole and waited in the woods. At sundown he piled his things on a point of land at the bend of the river. When it grew dark, he waded in like Half Arrow told him. The water was cold and he did not go far. After a while he called the call of the Schachachgokhos as they had agreed. But there was no reply, only the faint gurgling sounds in the river.

He had given up calling and almost hope when the impatient whoo-haw of the barred owl sounded in the river. Quickly he answered and waded farther out. Presently in the darkness he made out a shadow approaching over the water. When it reached him, he found a wet and dripping Half Arrow in a dugout but it was not the larger.

"The big one has an iron rope," Half Arrow told him.

"Let's be glad the trader hadn't two iron ropes," True Son said. He pulled the boat to shore and made haste to load it with their things. Then quickly he climbed in and they shoved off.

All night they lay floating on the current of the Alleghi Sipu, listening for falls ahead, peering through the darkness to avoid rocks and logs, poling quickly to the side at shallows and Indian fish weirs. Before daylight they pulled the dugout into hiding on the thickly wooded shore, smoothing the telltale marks in the mud. All day they lay hidden, resting, watching the boats that went up and down. When no one was in sight, they split strips from a fallen pine and whittled them into paddles. After nightfall they were on the river again.

It was just before daylight when Half Arrow woke him with a sharp word of caution.

"*Nechil*" he said.

Looking ahead, True Son glimpsed a dull red campfire winking from the western shore. Then suddenly to the east there came into view the dark outlines of a settlement dotted already at this early hour with two or three burning candles and wood fires. Almost at once it flew into True Son's head where they were. Every moment he felt surer from the gleam of more water beyond.

"It's the great fort of the Plantscheman that is now of the Yengwes!" he whispered to Half Arrow.

It was risky to pass, they told each other, but still more risky to stop and camp. Here the half-white, half-Indian trader and even the men from Peshtank might be waiting. Lying tense and low in the boat, they rode the gauntlet through. Never, True Son told his cousin, would he forget this morning in the Month That the Deer Turns Red, with the sight of Fort Pitt standing bristling on the point of land between the two rivers, its lights small and few, its strong stockade, redoubts and houses dark and sinister against the faint murky streaks of red and orange in the eastern sky.

"The last time I saw it, I was heavy and a prisoner," he said. "Now I go light and free."

Then their dugout sped silently to the great meeting of the waters and passed into the sweep of the Ohio beyond.

*xiii*

**O**NCE the ominous point of Fort Pitt was past, they hid their boat and selves by day no longer.

"Indian world now," Half Arrow said. "Nobody comes after us here."

All that day they drifted with the current, paddling a little from either shore where white landspies, travelling where they had no right, might covet their dugout. Most of the time they lay back dozing in the sun, for last night they had little sleep. Opening their eyes, they feasted on the passing richness of the Indian forest. Mile after mile it stood, untouched as the Great One had made it. Here were no roads bringing a plague of Yengwe carts, no prison fields, no unjust fences, no clocks enslaving the sun. Once a flock of noisy paroquets with the bright feathers that warriors coveted flew overhead. Where small rivers flowed into the larger, they saw the good bark shelter of Indian camps and villages. Twice canoes shot out to hail them in their own tongue for news from the English fort. All the while, there was before them the constant wheeling unfoldment of the river.

At sunset the deserted mouth of a creek drew them in. Cautiously they paddled up to find a place for the night.

The great butts of the forest stood on either hand guarding the watery glade. It was utterly still. Only the drip from the lifted paddles ringed the glassy water. The last slanting rays of their father, the Sun, laid a red benediction upon them. Then suddenly the thick darkness of the forest fell.

What kind of place it was they could not be sure of till morning. When it came, they found themselves lying on a ferny bank looking up through a lofty network of branches. Their father, the Sun, was back, smiling on them. The whole beautiful day lay ahead. There was no mist. All their little world stood in the crystal clarity of early forest morning. Their sister-in-law, the Creek, crept slowly past them. Their brother-in-law, the South Wind, rippled her with his breath.

"It's a place prepared for us," True Son said. "We mustn't offend the Preparer by going away without tasting it."

"I think the Preparer knows our corn meal is gone from the sack," Half Arrow agreed.

They set to work on a brush net at once. Often had they seen their fathers at the task. First they laid down the pliant new whips of the soft maple. Then they gathered vines from the forest grape, the Five Fingers and other creepers. Weaving them in and out of the branches, they tied each with a knot as it passed through. It took most of the hungry day. Then their brush seine was ready. It was not so large as they had hoped. It looked still smaller dragged behind the dugout. The little fish swam through it. But the second time they drew it out, two longish white moons came rising from the watery depths, and soon a pair of big and shiny fish threw themselves about on the ferny bank.

Half Arrow's fierce shout of joy whooped through the woods.

"Now already I am strong!" he cried.

They didn't leave next day or the next. As boys in the village, this was the fortune they had dreamed about, the greatest boon the Lord of Heaven could give them, a life of fishing and hunting, forgetting all else and by all else forgot, abandoning themselves to the forest and the bounty of its wild beasts. Always up to now they had gone as wards and lackeys of their fathers. Now at last they were their own masters. No one stood between them and life. They took their joy and meat direct from its hand.

They passed their days in a kind of primitive deliciousness. The past was buried. There was only the present and tomorrow. By day they lived as happy animals. Moonlight nights in the forest they saw what the deer saw. Swimming under water with open eyes, they knew now what the otter knew.

The change in the weather was always foretold them by their uncle, the Moon. They could hear the rain before it reached them, a fine unmistakable roar in the forest. They lay snug under the upturned dugout, watching the trees drink in the wetness. Sometimes it thundered on their wooden roof. Then they knew it was a shower and soon over. But some days it fell with a long, soft, beautiful sound through the woods, so light at times they only knew it continued by the leaves on trees and bushes delicately nodding. The great butts turned darker with the wet. The mold under foot grew browner. Roots above ground were always black enough. Now they looked blacker. Nothing but their brother-in-law, the East Wind, moved among the trees. After a long day of rain it seemed that this small dry spot where they lay was the only place left on earth. All the rest of the world did not exist, had never been.

But next morning after the rain, the mist drifted through the woods, vanishing like smoke, and they knew that all the drowned and blotted-out world was freshly

created again. The mosses and trailing pine, the winter-
green, the mats of arbutus and partridge berry had never
been so new and green. Lichens stood up risen from the
dead. You walked the thick leaves from last fall and
underfoot there was no sound. Neither was there mud
like in the white man's fields and roads. The forest floor
lay clean and springy from ancient logs long since rotted
level with the ground and now returned to a kind of
youth by the rain from heaven.

When the two boys tired of fishing, they gathered shag
bark and pine knots. Then they waited for a night when
their uncle, the Moon, lay abed. First they set a clump of
freshly picked branches in the dugout's bow. Behind it
sat Half Arrow holding high a blazing torch of bark and
pine tied by creepers. In the rear behind a second clump
of green leaves, True Son paddled silently. His rifle lay
ready across the thwarts. The fire lighted up the road of
the creek through the forest like day. They saw coons
illumined and transfixed at the water's edge where they
hunted frogs and crayfish. The boat glided through an
unreal world. Submerged logs like Water Bulls of the
Southern rivers passed below them. Above them from
either side trees mingled the white bellies of their leaves
while before them on the forest bank a buck, with jaws
adrip from his drink, waited for the fatal bullet.

Part of each day they squatted by the fire, cutting each
other's ears to make them seemly, pulling the other's un-
necessary hair, their wet fingers dipped in ashes. Only
the long center growth on the head was left hanging.
They were in no hurry, drifting with the day, mingling
with slow time. Always the fertile forest spread around
them. Abundance supported them. Completeness was for
the taking. Days unfolded, rich and inexhaustible. After
the Month When the Deer Turns Red came the Honey
Bee Month. Soon would follow the Month When Corn
Is in the Milk. Even though they wished it, they couldn't

stay forever. Their families would be wondering. They hated to go but they hated worse to stay. The sun had passed its northern meridian and was beginning its slow return. The foliage of the great forest wall had turned from light green to dark. It was time to leave.

The first thing they did when at last they reached the mouth of the Muskingum was to bathe in the home waters. And now as they paddled north there opened up before them the sacred heart of their Indian country, the beloved Forks of the Muskingum. Hurrying from the northwest came the White Woman's River and from the northeast sprang the brave Tuscarawas. From here on the two boys never halted. Every bank and sandbar was familiar until they rounded the final bend and there among the great trees stood the bark village with blue smoke rising from the high pitched roofs, with the forms of home villagers moving among the cabins and the sun throwing long shadows across the river over bank and street. It was as True Son had seen it so often in his mind, but never had he trembled like this at the sight.

They heard dogs barking at the strange dugout and saw brown faces turn toward them while quick hands shielded eyes from the sun. They had a glimpse of Shangas, the Exhorter, already dressed in his buffalo head and bearskins to preach against evil to whomsoever would listen. And there lounging easily with his pipe was Nischa, strong as two men, with Wapahamink, his crippled son who drew himself backward on the ground; and Nungasa, the girl whom True Son used always to find looking so steadily at him; and Moschaigeu, the old scalped one who wore a rag of beaver to cover his ancient wound; and Tsuchechin, the fat squaw who had once defended True Son, hiding him from a beating when his father and uncle were away; and Suskit, the big black dog that always wanted to go with him; and Wikiwon, who had a difficulty of speech and was mocked by boys singing war songs through their noses.

"Now they know us and run to tell our cabins!" Half Arrow exulted. By the time they beached the dugout, a little group of squaws and young people stood smiling and chattering to them from the high bank. The two youths answered with fitting restraint. Weren't they men now, and hunters, home from an alien land? With dignity they picked up their belongings and stalked up the bank, trying to see no farther to the right or left than they had to.

"True Son, is it really you!" a soft voice hailed him, and there was his younger sister, A'astonah, her long hair streaming behind her, running with the children who had come to the cabin.

True Son looked at her with love and aloofness, carrying his rifle, passing her by, striding on with Half Arrow, past his older sister, Mechelit, who stood halfway with bright vermillion cloth in her black hair, on to the door of his cabin where his mother waited. He saw her look of joy and that she had quickly fastened buckles to her strouding at news of his coming, but now she drew back to let him pass first to his father who stood straight in the shadows. Cuyloga's face was strong and impassive. Not a line could you read from its muscles, but from his eyes True Son thought he discerned a deep welcome. Here in the shelter of the cabin, while others who had the right crowded in and many eyes watched from the doorway, they embraced.

"*Elke!* Do you live yet, True Son! And are you come home to stay?" his father said, breathing heavily.

TRUE SON slept that night in the bosom of his family. He lay at his accustomed place. He felt close around him the presence and affections of those dear to him. The good awareness of their rich brown skin, of their gray deer hide and bright calico garments, the rise and fall of their breath pervaded him. Familiar Indian odors of family and cabin that had been part of him since childhood lulled him to sleep. Even in unconsciousness he knew them. They spoke to his heart. They said now it could beat softly and at ease, for he was home again.

For several days the village celebrated the boys' return. The cabins of True Son's father and uncle stood open to friends to come and share their rejoicing. The delicacies of bear's oil and tree sugar were poured on hominy and venison and offered to the men. Warriors and hunters went from one house to the other, visiting, smoking, eating up all the two houses had. They shook bowls of plum stones for dice, the stones painted black on one side and white on the other. The sounds of their calling for black or white and then of their loud and triumphant counting could be heard through the village. There were the twanging of jew's harps and the high whistling of hollowed cane flutes. True Son had thought nothing could approach the joy of hunting in the forest. But now he felt contentment in the deep summer days of the village. Afterwards they seemed to him like a dream.

It was a dream even then with shadows in it. Each day he was aware that not all the men of the village joined in the festivities. The cousins of Little Crane, who lived only a stone's throw away, did not come. They sat on a log in a group with their cronies and refrained from greeting True Son when he passed.

"If we had fetched back your white uncle's scalp, this would not have happened," Half Arrow spoke in True Son's ear. "But take no notice. My father says it will pass. Time will dry it up like carrion."

Just the same both boys felt uneasiness when the brother of Little Crane came from the Killbuck. His name was Thitpan, which means Bitter, and his mouth was puckered up as from a mocker nut. With him were High Bank, his father-in-law, with only one eye; and Niskitoon, which means Put-on-Paint, whose skin was tattooed from head to foot with signs of valor; also others, including Cheek Bone, a Shawano. They carried rifles, mallets, tomahawks, packs for the trail, and an old keg. One end of the latter had been knocked out and deer hide stretched over. With Thitpan's cousins they took up in the council house, which stood very near the cabin of Cuyloga. Here they started beating the drum.

True Son knew instantly from his father's face that this was serious. Not often had he seen his father so unbent and even jovial as since he had returned to him. But now his father's joking and easy bearing were gone. Grimly he listened to the drum and the songs for vengeance and war.

"When will the white man learn!" he muttered. "He says to the Indian, brother, have peace. The Indian buries the tomahawk. He hides it deep under a stump. He believes his brother, the white man. He visits his brother, the white man. Then his brother, the white man, murders him, a guest under his roof. He thinks no more of it than killing a snake in his cabin. The white man talks to other Indians. He says, brother, what's the matter? Why do you go to war? Why dig up the tomahawk? *Ekih!* The white man is a strange creature of the Almighty. He is hard to fathom. How can you reason with him? He is like a spoiled child without instruction. He has no understanding of good and evil."

Sumakek, Black Fish, the father of Half Arrow, nodded. But True Son, standing with his cousin behind the men, could feel his mother and sisters stir uneasily at the talk and at the cries of recruiting.

"Look this way!" Little Crane's brother kept calling from the council house. "The cause of my brother is loud! It cries for blood! It's high in the sight of Heaven!"

"It's not necessary for everybody to join," True Son's mother ventured in the cabin.

"No, but I am not everybody," her brother, Black Fish, answered. "My son was Little Crane's companion. He walked with him on the journey when he was scalped. How can I turn my back?"

"Your back and mine are too broad to turn," Cuyloga agreed gravely. "It was going to visit my son that Little Crane was deprived of his life. *Ekih!* In my son's own white village."

"If you go, you wouldn't take True Son and Half Arrow along! They are only boys!" his mother begged them.

There was no answer from the two fathers. Behind their backs, Half Arrow and True Son exchanged glances. Anyone could see they were bursting to go. When the war party in the council house sang its war songs, both were filled with excitement. The chanting

moved them so that scarcely could they contain themselves at the fearful scalp yells that followed. The long
Ow-w-w-w-w-w turning into a sudden uw-w-w-w-w-
w-w-w-w and held on a fierce tingling note set their
blood on fire. Eagerly to each other they made the swift
motions of tomahawking and scalping.

True Son's mother watched bitterly.

"Cuyloga. Think what the whites will do to our son if
they catch him. They will burn him as a traitor to their
side."

"Woman. Stay home and boil your pots," Cuyloga reproved her. "It is something I have no choice in. True
Son is nearly a man. It would not look good for him to
stay behind. Our friends would say he is surely white,
see he is unwilling to fight against his white people."

"*Bischi*," his brother-in-law grunted in agreement.

"But he needn't go unless he wants to," Cuyloga
added.

"I go!" True Son said quickly. He felt the flush of a
great exultation. He stood very straight, looking away
not to see the quick pain in his mother's and sisters'
faces. They were women and couldn't be expected to
understand.

Much was healed between the friends of Little Crane
and themselves when Cuyloga and Black Fish with their
sons joined. Now they were all brothers in arms against
the white murderers. Under-the-Hill, with an old purple
wound in his cheek, also joined, as did Pepallistank, Disbeliever, who with his bobbing lameness was about the
fastest on his feet in the village; and Kschippihelleu,
whose name in English was Strong Water; and several
others.

Now it is the custom that he who first proposes going
to war is the leader. As Thitpan did, the others followed.
When he tied up his pack, they tied up theirs. When he
took his musket, tomahawk and death mallet, the others

took up theirs. When he sang his war song of farewell and promise not to return save with scalps and captives, the others made the chorus of brave ferocity and deserving death noises that can't be spoken in words but only in memory sounds that have come down in the ancient deeds of the race. True Son felt a savage sweetness he had never known before. He saw before his eyes a redness that colored all things like blood. He tasted a violence wilder than any root or game. Then Thitpan led the way out of the council house, followed in a single line by the rest.

Half Arrow and True Son brought up the rear. The latter remembered how it had been when last he had left the village. Then with everybody watching as today, his mother and sisters, his aunt and cousins, his friends and neighbors, his father had dragged him off like a dog. Now he went as a warrior, painted, his eyebrows and hair plucked, on his back his small pack and in his hands his hatchet and striped rifle with brass fittings that was the envy of everybody who watched. Once out of sight of the village, Thitpan shot off his gun and the others followed in a blast of farewell and promise to those at home who listened.

As guide for the party, Thitpan chose Disbeliever. This was a slight on his father, the boy knew. Why, there was no greater He-Who-Knows-the-Marks in the forest than his father. He could follow the trail of the most careful and secretive stranger, sometimes naming both his tribe and age. More than once he had taught True Son his art, how to read the smallest sign on the ground or bushes, a leaf turned back or a blade of grass down, a bit of mud on a stone, gravel turned up, how in snow men would tread in each other's tracks to look like one instead of two or many.

But today his father betrayed no flicker of disappointment, and his son stayed impassive like him. In silence

he followed where Thitpan and Disbeliever led, on a
path neither he nor Half Arrow had ever trod before. By
the tree moss and slant of the sun, True Son knew they
traveled with the east wind on one side and the south
wind on the other. By a deep riffle they crossed the Ohio
and climbed hills strange to him.

In a forest valley they divided. One party under Black
Fish stayed on the path, and another with Thitpan, Cuyloga, and others turned to the south where Disbeliever
said were white men's cabins. They made out to meet at
a spring across the mountain. The two boys went with
the party under Black Fish.

Late that afternoon when all were met again, True
Son noticed at once that Thitpan's party carried booty
and something else. A leaping ran through his blood like
quicksilver as he saw their first scalps, one an ugly dark
roan like rusted iron, one brown streaked with gray and
a smaller one with long fine hair the color of willow
shoots in the spring.

"*Jukella!* Oh, that I had been a lucky one!" Half Arrow
wished.

By the fire that evening the two boys listened to a re-
cital of the battle. Not a detail was left out from the time
the Indians drew near the unlawful fields the white
people had cut from the Indian forest and the cabins
they had wrongfully built. The whole course of strata-
gem was recounted, every sign and movement, the
successful deception and ambush, all the fearful and
cowardly efforts of the whites to escape and appease
them, together with the foolish and fruitless words they
cried in their religion which was no help to them now.

Eagerly the two boys watched the takers of the scalps
skillfully dry them, stretching them on red hoops and
trimming off the uneven pieces with their knives. Each
time a piece was dropped, Half Arrow picked it up.
With deerhide thread he sewed a small, pied, makeshift

scalp for himself. The two boys put it on a pole and danced around it, singing fierce words of scorn and victory. But all the time the tender pieces of discarded scalp with long soft hairs the color of willow shoots in the spring kept entering True Son's blood like long worms clotting the free wild flow. He tried to forget what he had said to his white mother, that never had he seen a child's scalp taken by his Indian people.

Before he lay down for the night, he spoke to his father.

"Then the very young of the whites are our enemies, too?" he asked.

His father did not answer, only sat there strong with a look of aloofness, as if to say this was none of his doing. But Thitpan, who claimed the young scalp, answered angrily.

"They are our enemies, yes. Was my brother young or old? *Bischi*, he was not much more than a youth and yet he was murdered by your white uncle."

"It is clear to me now, cousin," True Son said humbly. "I ask you to forget my ignorance. I did not know we fought children."

To his surprise, his words produced a murmur of disapproval.

"Young cousin. I don't fight children. On our way home I should have taken her prisoner. But a child holds us back on our way forward. Young cousin. It was lighter for us to carry her scalp than her body."

True Son said nothing more, but he was conscious of dark eyes resentful at criticism from a boy.

Next day they came on a wide river. When Under-the-Hill joined them from downstream, he said that a boat of whites had just passed. Had they been an hour earlier they might have enticed it to shore and enriched themselves with rifles and powder. His report enlivened the eyes of the warriors. They held quick council. They would wait for another boat. This was a favorite river to the whites. Many from the Quekel provinces used it as a watery road to the west. Sometimes traders and even settlers, seeking to steal Indian lands, could be found floating on it.

"Now your son will be good for something," Thitpan said to Cuyloga. "Tomorrow he can call in his white cousins. When the boat comes close, we will fall on them with lead and hatchet."

It was strange, True Son thought to himself, that here among his Indian brothers this night he should dream of his white father and mother. He saw them in his dream as clear and real as in life. It was wintertime in the dream and their sled hunted him in the forest. "Johnny! Johnny!" they called as the sled went over the snowy ground. Then suddenly the sled was a boat, the snow was water and other white people stood with his parents in the boat. For the first time he saw that a white child was with his mother. He tried to see the face of the child, but it kept looking the other way. It was afraid of something. At last True Son heard what it heard, the roar of Sokpehellak, the waterfall, just ahead of them on the river.

True Son woke in a sweat. He could still clearly see his white father's bulging head, the high cloak around the shoulders of his mother and the frightened crouch of the child.

In the morning, Thitpan and Disbeliever instructed the boy in the meritorious art of decoy. First they had him wade in the river and wash off his war paint with sand. Then they bade him pull on a pair of pantaloons they had taken from one of the white cabins. The legs were too long and the warriors gravely consulted what to do. In the end they cut them short with their knives. Also, the blouse they gave him to wear was wrong. Perhaps it had belonged to the slain girl. It was too small and constrained him. He showed them he could scarcely move his arms or shoulders in it, but they told him what mattered only was that he look like a white boy. The smaller he looked, the better to melt the whites' cruel and stony hearts. Then Disbeliever took Cheek Bone along up the river to watch.

All day True Son waited for word that a boat was in sight. But the day passed and the next, and the only creatures that passed on the river were Those-Which-Go-Self-Suspended, the birds, and Those-Which-Go-Crooked, the butterflies. By the third day Thitpan said they had waited long enough. They took a vote to cross the river, but then Disbeliever, who had never deserted his post, came running and hopping down the path. He said a large flatboat of whites had just hove around the upper bend. Hurriedly True Son was given back his pantaloons to cover his breechclout. He was helped on with his white blouse and sent into the river.

"Remember," Thitpan instructed him, "you are not Lenape now. You are white. You must talk and act white. You must make their foolish white hearts bleed so they come close to help you."

The water felt mild enough as he waded in, and yet the boy found himself shivering. He had to stand in the river a long time. Once or twice he thought Disbeliever might have mistaken a floating log for a distant boat of white people. When he looked back to shore he could see nothing. Thitpan had picked a place where the bank was thick with wipochk. Not a wisp of smoke arose, nor was there a sign of life among the bushes. Even the footprints on the bank had been smoothed out. The river shore looked peaceful and unpeopled as the deepest forest. Then he turned back to the water and saw an actual boat pushing around the bend above him.

It was larger than he expected, filled with white people and their possessions. For a moment the thought of all the scalps and plunder gave his blood a fierce upward surge. Surely some should be allotted to him, for without him the others could do nothing. In his mind he recounted Yengwe words to call.

He felt sure that the boat had seen him. At first when it cleared the bend, it had kept to the middle of the river as if to be reasonably safe from either shore. But now he could see it pushing farther away from him. Although still a distance off, he lifted his empty hands and sent Yengwe words across the water.

"Brothers. Help! Brothers. I am English. I have white skin like you!"

The boat slowed visibly. There were both oars and poles among the men, but their use was suspended now. With its passengers staring, the craft drifted on the current. Presently it had lessened its distance enough for True Son to recognize the dress of several women.

"Mothers! Take me with you! Mothers! See, I am white boy! Mothers! Take me or I starve."

He called so piteously that now he could hear the voice of one of the women remonstrating with the unwilling men. He couldn't make out the words, but her tone had the same imperial quality of his white mother when she forced her wishes on his white father.

"Brothers. Listen to her!" he cried. "Mothers. Don't pass by!"

Slowly he saw the boat make its first movement toward him. A man's harsh voice shouted to him.

"If you're white, wade out to the middle and we'll pick you up."

True Son waded only a little farther. He crouched low in the water making it seem to cover his shoulders.

"Is deep! I can't swim!" he whimpered.

He could hear the burden of argument rising from the boat and understand most of the words. Some believed in him and wanted to pick him up. Others shouted to the

boatman to go on. They mistrusted this strange youth in
the river. Why did he say Brothers and Mothers, like the
savages, and why was his hair cut around the edges in
the Indian fashion? Why hadn't he chosen a shallow
place where he could wade out? The man with the harsh
voice declared he would come no closer even though the
boy had a Bible in his hands. But one of the women was
True Son's friend. She called them cowards. She said
with spirit that if they were afraid to pick him up, she
would take an oar and do it herself.

Some of the men gave in to her. Little by little the
heavily loaded flatboat slanted across the river. At his
back True Son could feel the rising exultation of his
hidden friends. Then someone in the boat moved and
disclosed a child. It was a boy about Gordie's age,
dressed in a dark gray dress with a broad light band
around it such as his small white brother used to wear.
True Son stared and his begging abruptly ceased. Like a
flash he remembered his dream. Could it be that his
white father and mother were on this boat, coming west
to find him, and that they had taken Gordie along? For
the moment he forgot who and where he was. He was
conscious only of this child so like Gordie coming closer
and closer to the unseen rifles and tomahawks of his
companions.

Once the child spoke to its mother and at the sound
of the slender voice, True Son felt himself shaken.

"Take him back! It's an ambush!" he suddenly
screamed.

For a moment the men on the boat stood startled.
True Son saw terror and incredulity on the face of the
white woman. Then in a panic the men bent their oars
and poles to return the boat out of range. When it was
seen that the prize was escaping, a volley of Indian shots
rang out. True Son ducked as bullets went over him. He
saw a stout man in the boat fall back as if too gross a

mark to be missed. But distance kept most of the shots from taking effect. While the Indians came out on the bank yelling, reloading and firing again, the boat made off downstream, hugging the farther bank.

*xv*

NOT until the boy turned back to shore did he realize the gravity of what he had done. He had betrayed his own brothers. None had welcome for him as he climbed the bank. Even Half Arrow turned away. Thitpan especially looked down on him angry and grim.

"Why don't you go with your friends? Why come back to us?" he asked scornfully.

True Son didn't answer. What could he say that they would understand? He didn't understand himself. He stood wet and miserable while the warriors withdrew to discuss him, his father and uncle among them. From time to time he caught the words: *tipatit,* chicken; *achgook,* snake; *putschiskey,* poison vine; *schwannack,* bad white people; and *schupijaw,* spy. When he started to take off his dripping blouse, Thitpan called to him angrily.

"It is fitting to a white person. Let it stay."

"It is wet and cold," True Son told him.

"Maybe soon it will be dry and hot enough," Thitpan promised.

He spoke to Disbeliever and Under-the-Hill, who seized the boy. They bound his hands and feet with creepers. Then they let him stand. Disbeliever took charcoal from the fire and blacked half of True Son's face. Under-the-Hill fetched white clay from the river bank. With this he chalked the remaining side.

The boy knew well what it meant. They were divided in council about him, were going to try him in the Lenape fashion. Here in their court under the roof of the Indian forest they would decide his fate, whether to do to him as the charcoal signified or let him remain alive. Thitpan and his cousins were for burning. True Son, they said, had been sent by the white people. His tongue was like the crooked stripes of the whites' talking papers. His heart would always be with the whites. There was no Indian blood in him.

True Son stood hearing, waiting. It was strange that, with all their talk of his white badness, never had he felt more Indian than at this moment. All the stories he knew of his Indian people who with calmness of mind accepted their death sentence came to his mind. He remembered Be-Smoke, whom the Lenni Lenape gave a reprieve of two years to live among his own clan, the Unamis. Easily he might have stayed away the rest of his life but came back on the prescribed day for his execution. Also there was Heavy Belt freed at night by his brothers-in-law but who stayed to die because it had been decreed against him by the village. True Son understood them perfectly. How could life mean anything to you if already your people had killed you in their minds?

Thitpan voted first, throwing a heavy stick on the fire to show his strong choice for burning. One after another followed, tossing sticks. When he saw how it was going, Half Arrow turned and stumbled off in the forest. True Son in pity watched him disappear among the leaves. His own father, he noticed, waited as if till last. When it came to the turn of his uncle, Black Fish, the latter motioned his brother-in-law to go ahead, signifying he would vote with him.

The boy's father stood there a moment. Then deliberately he went to the fire. True Son's heart sank. He felt sure that his father joined in the vote against him. Then he saw that his father carried no stick. Instead he picked up a charred one from the fire. Silently he began blacking his own face, not one side, but both and the backs of the hands also. When he was done, he faced them.

All had watched him puzzled and a little disquieted. Now they waited, fastening their eyes on him. Cuyloga looked powerful and forbidding, his eyes in the black face flashing with whiteness.

"Brothers," he spoke. "I have listened to the council. I hear that my son is a spy from the whites, that his tongue is the fork of a tree and his heart black. Brothers. You know me. I am Cuyloga. Cuyloga knows his son. It was Cuyloga who raised and instructed him. He is like Cuyloga. If he is double-tongued and a spy, then Cuyloga is also. Why don't you bind and burn Cuyloga, for he is the father and responsible for the bad instruction?"

There was only a kind of displeasure and uneasiness from his hearers. Cuyloga went on. Never had he appeared more formidable and magnificent to his son than at this moment.

"Brothers. What do you expect of me—to stand idly by while you burn my son? My son has brought death to none of us. The scratches he gave us are not on our bodies but our pride. Brothers. How if my son is burnt do I go back and face her who lives with me in my house? How do I look in the eyes of his sisters who think the rainbow arches over him? Brothers. It is easier for me to fight you all than go back and say that Cuyloga stood by and did nothing while his brothers in anger put his son to the fire."

With the quickness of Long Tail, the panther, he took his knife and cut the boy's thongs. Then he stood there waiting for the attack but none came. The warriors were too astonished. They watched, sullen and yet fascinated by the drama. This was the great Cuyloga at his bravest that they looked upon, and none knew what he would do next.

When he saw that they hesitated to fight him, he turned to the boy. His manner was not softened. He spoke, if anything, with sterner dignity.

"True Son. I have things also to say to you. It is not easy to say them. When you were very small, I took you in. I adopted you in my family. You were to me like my own son. I taught you to speak with a straight tongue. I showed you right and wrong. I bound you to my heart with strong new vines. The old rotten vines that held you to the white people I tore apart. True Son. Now I find these old rotten vines have new life. They have sprouted again to pull you back to the white people.

"True Son. From your early days you were not neglected. You were taught the kinds and signs of game. You were taught their habits and where to find them. You were taught to hunt and shoot. You gave me no shame as a hunter. I told myself that when I am old, you, my son, will support me. When my bones creak, you will keep me in bear's oil and venison. When the ashes of life cool, you will be the fire to warm my old age. Never did I think that you would turn against me and that I would have to send you back to your white people. All this time I looked on you as Indian. I leaned on you as a staff. Now it is broken."

True Son heard with emotion.

"My father. Never will I go back to the whites. They

are strange to me. They are my enemies. My father. If you send me away, I must go, but never to the white people."

His father looked at him with sternness and pity for a long time.

"True Son. Maybe not now, you think. But after you are away from us for a while, you will go back. True Son. I look into your heart. I look into your head. I look into your blood. Your heart is Indian. Your head is Indian. But your blood is still thin like the whites. It can be joined only with the thin blood of the white people. It does not mix with the brave redness of Indian blood. True Son. I and you must leave here together. When we come to a white man's road, that will be the place of our parting. You must go one way. I must go the other. Afterwards the path will be closed between us. True Son. On the way to that road, no harm will come to you. Cuyloga will watch over his son. After that road, we are son and father no longer. We are not even cousins but enemies. You must have no pity for me or I for you. When sometime you meet me in battle, you must kill me, for that is what I must do to you."

The boy's mouth was stopped. He could say nothing, only look at his parent whom he had never loved or yearned for so much as at this moment. From behind a bush where he had returned, he saw Half Arrow's look of bitter emotion. Even Little Crane's brother and cousins had been powerfully moved by the scene and oration. What they might do to his father in ambush later, he could not guess, but there would be no attempt to molest either of them now.

At a sign from his father, True Son kept on the white blouse and pantaloons. Both gathered up their packs. There was no leavetaking. The two boys looked at each other a long farewell. Cuyloga had already left and True Son moved up the riverbank path after him.

In the afternoon, Cuyloga shot a turkey. They roasted and ate it before evening. The boy could hardly touch it and he thought that the meat stuck in his father's mouth also. Near noon next day they came to a ford. A wide trail led down from the north and crossed the river. With a sickening feeling, the boy saw the track was rutted by white men's carts.

His father spoke bleakly.

"This is the parting place. This is where the path must be closed between us. My place is on this side. Your place is on that. You must never cross it. If you come back, I cannot receive you and they will kill you."

The boy stood there a long time. He knew his father was waiting for him to go. At last he made the first movement, but at the edge of the water he turned. He hoped he would see in his father the faintest sign of relenting, but he found only fixed purpose in those dark eyes.

"My father. Do we say good-by to each other now?"

"Enemies do not do so," Cuyloga told him harshly. "I am no longer your father, nor you my son."

"Then who is my father?" the boy cried in despair and turned quickly to hide the blinding wetness in his eyes.

There was no reply from behind him. After a moment he forced himself into the water. It came to him then that this was the second time he was made to go through this living death. Not a year ago had he been forced to part from Half Arrow and Little Crane. Then, like his father today, they had stayed on the afternoon side of the river. Then he had felt the same bitter grief as now. Then as today he was made against his will to take up his life among the white people.

But gladly would he exchange today for yesterday, if he only could. Then, no matter the ordeal, he could always go back. Then Half Arrow and Little Crane had waited faithfully on the bank while he crossed. So long as his trail ran by the water, he had seen them still standing on the afternoon side, raising their hands to him in loyalty and affection. But today when he came to the morning side and turned, no one stood watching him from the distant shore. His father was gone. He stood alone in the forest by the river.

Ahead of him ran the rutted road of the whites. It led, he knew, to where men of their own volition constrained themselves with heavy clothing like harness, where men chose to be slaves to their own or another's property and followed empty and desolate lives far from the wild beloved freedom of the Indian.

## ABOUT THE AUTHOR

CONRAD RICHTER was born in Pennsylvania, the son, grandson, nephew, and great-nephew of clergymen. He was intended for the ministry, but at thirteen he declined a scholarship and left preparatory school for high school, from which he was graduated at fifteen. After graduation he went to work. His family on his mother's side was identified with the early American scene, and from boyhood on he was saturated with tales and the color of Eastern pioneer days. In 1928 he and his small family moved to New Mexico, where his heart and mind were soon captured by the Southwest. From this time on he devoted himself to fiction. *The Sea of Grass* and *The Trees* were awarded the gold medal of the Societies of Libraries of New York University in 1942. *The Town* received the Pulitzer Prize in 1951, and *The Waters of Kronos* won the 1960 National Book Award for fiction. His other novels include *The Fields* (1946), *The Light in the Forest* (1953), *The Lady* (1957), *A Simple Honorable Man* (1962), *The Grandfathers* (1964), and *The Aristocrat*, published just before his death in 1968.